Praise for Norma Klein and THAT'S MY BABY

"A warm and funny coming-of-age story set against a strong contemporary background . . . When it comes to young adult books, Klein has shown herself to be a writer of great wit and charm."
Publishers Weekly

"Klein's latest bittersweet portrayal of contemporary adolescence will delight readers. . . . Klein tells this story realistically and sympathetically."
Library Journal

"She has a great knack for creating characters of warmth and likability. She is sharp and perceptive, but kind. She knows what makes people tick, but forgives their idiosyncracies."
The Boston Globe

"Neatly and convincingly, Klein handles the question of the plausibility of Paul and Zoe's romance. Issues of censorship, stepparenting, friendship, and sexuality add texture to this coming-of-age story."
ALA Booklist

Also by Norma Klein:

GIVE ME ONE GOOD REASON
TAKING SIDES
BLUE TREES, RED SKY
LOVE AND OTHER EUPHEMISMS (stories)*
CONFESSIONS OF AN ONLY CHILD
GOING BACKWARDS
HIDING
MOM, THE WOLFMAN, AND ME
NAOMI IN THE MIDDLE
WHAT IT'S ALL ABOUT
BREAKING UP
A HONEY OF A CHIMP
TOMBOY
ROBBIE AND THE LEAP YEAR BLUES
IT'S NOT WHAT YOU EXPECT
THE QUEEN OF WHAT IFS*
BEGINNERS' LOVE*
DOMESTIC ARRANGEMENTS*
IT'S OK IF YOU DON'T LOVE ME*
LOVE IS ONE OF THE CHOICES*
SUNSHINE
WIVES AND OTHER WOMEN
BIZOU*
COMING TO LIFE*
THE SWAP
SEXTET IN A MINOR (stories)
ANGEL FACE*
SNAPSHOTS*
LOVERS
GIRLS TURN WIVES*
THE CHEERLEADER*
GIVE AND TAKE*
FAMILY SECRETS*
OLDER MEN*
AMERICAN DREAMS
MY LIFE AS A BODY*
NO MORE SATURDAY NIGHTS*

*Published by Fawcett Books

THAT'S MY BABY

Norma Klein

FAWCETT JUNIPER • NEW YORK

RLI: $\underline{\text{VL 6 & up}}$
IL 10 & up

A Fawcett Juniper Book
Published by Ballantine Books
Copyright © 1988 by Norma Klein

Library of Congress Catalog Card Number: 87-40442

ISBN 0-449-70356-8

This edition published by arrangement with Viking Penguin, a division of Penguin Books USA Inc.

Grateful acknowledgement is made for permission to reprint "i like my body when it is with yours" from *Tulips & Chimneys* by e. e. cummings. Copyright 1923, 1925 and renewed 1951, 1953 by e. e. cummings. Copyright © 1973, 1976 by the Trustees for the e. e. cummings Trust. Copyright © 1973, 1976 by George James Firmage. Reprinted by permission of Liveright Publishing Corporation.

Manufactured in the United States of America

First Ballantine Books Edition: May 1990

For Steven Kroll

CHAPTER 1

As luck would have it, I didn't meet Sonya on the way to school. In fact, we somehow managed not to meet all day, which isn't as strange as it sounds since our senior class at Hamilton has 250 students. Also, senior year is set up a little oddly at our school. They figured that since most kids spend senior year waiting to hear what college they've gotten into and not caring that much about their classes, they would just dispense with some classes altogether. You just have to take two, or maybe three if you're a glutton for punishment. The rest of the time you get, or try and get, a job. This varies from pure money-making—e.g., working at David's Cookies—to (this happens about once in a million) getting a job connected with what you think will be your life's work.

I want to be a playwright. Notice, I say I want to. I know it may not work out. I know the odds. But that's why I decided to take a job as a salesclerk in a small bookstore in Soho. The pay is nothing, but I'll be learning a few basic skills. It might give me something to do in the lean years before my first big hit arrives. Better than being a waiter, anyway. Sometimes it seems like every waiter in New York City is a would-be something else.

I'll get to why I was trying to avoid Sonya, in time. It wasn't totally paranoid, though it's true that what happened took place last May and it's now September. Quite possibly it's all past history to her. You've got to hope, right? Then, as I was entering our apartment building, I saw Sonya's back. (She lives in the same apartment house as I do.) She was leafing through the mail which the doorman sticks in little wooden cubbyholes in the lobby. This *will* sound paranoid, but there was something about Sonya's back, the way she stood there, that made me realize she hadn't forgotten, that if, without turning around, she could have pressed a little button and eradicated me from the face of the earth, she'd probably have done it immediately. I stood there, half-frozen to the spot with guilt, anxiety, and some stupid, half-formed hope that my mind was just working overtime as usual. She turned.

"Hi, Paul," she said in her flat, dry Sonya-ish voice. Describe Sonya. Okay, here goes. The reason it's hard is this: we've known each other since seventh grade when we were both twelve. Half of me sees Sonya as she looks right now at eighteen, and half of me sees her as she looked then. What you have to know about "then" is that at twelve, I was entering Hamilton, whereas Sonya had been there since she was five. It's a public school for "intellectually gifted" kids and the only times you can enter are nursery school and seventh grade. So Sonya was an old-timer, had tons of friends, while I was a short, pudgy, weird-looking kid with one eye that wandered (that's since been corrected by surgery). No one would even recognize me now. I'm tall and handsome, of course. Actually, I *have* changed in major ways, some physical. I'm over six feet tall, for one. My father, Phil, says I grow every time he turns around. But everything hasn't quite fallen into place yet. My arms and legs have a peculiar gangling way of hanging there like I'm a cross between an ape and a scarecrow, and my hair, which is still wiry and blond, doesn't seem to know whether to lie down or stand straight on end, so it does some of each, depending on its mood. I don't even wear glasses anymore, by the way; I have contacts.

But—yes, I remember—I was going to describe Sonya. People used to say she looked like my sister, which made her furious—rightly so, I guess. What they meant was that she too has thick, frizzy blonde hair and big, hazel, slightly bulging eyes, only she doesn't wear, and never did, either glasses or contacts. She used to be short and a little pudgy, not quite so bad as I was, and is now skinny and definitely attractive, in an intense, intellectual kind of way. But what they probably also meant was manner. Sonya shoots from the hip, verbally. She claims she does it with me out of self-defense. I claim the same thing about her. Maybe we're both right.

"Have a good summer?" I asked, really friendly, probably suspiciously so. The last time we'd talked, she'd been going to be an au pair girl for an English family in Hampshire.

"Yeah, it was okay." She scooped up the mail, then pointed to Phil's box. "Want to take yours?"

"No, I'll leave it for Phil. . . . There's probably nothing for me, is there?"

"How should I know? I don't look through your mail every day!"

Whoops. First error of the conversation. We started strolling through our gigantic lobby to the elevator. "Was the, uh, family nice?" Sonya had been afraid the father might make a pass at her, as evidently middle-aged guys frequently do with teenage girls.

"Yeah, they were okay. . . . The mother was a little weird. She'd had some kind of breakdown and was a born-again Christian. So I heard a lot of stuff on hellfire and damnation."

"Did she convert you, or vice versa?"

"No. I figured she needed a cause, and who was I to shoot holes into her beliefs?"

That's unusual. Usually Sonya likes nothing better than shooting holes into people's beliefs. I refrained from pointing this out. "How about the father? You were worried."

3

Sonya wrinkled her arched, delicate nose. "No, I think he was a little—leaning toward bi, maybe. Just a feeling I got."

A pause. Not a Pinteresque pause, just a plain, awkward, what-do-we-say-now pause. If this were a year ago, I'd have said, "Did you meet anyone? Any guys?" Because a year ago Sonya and I were good friends. She's the only girl I've ever talked to about life, sex, parents, all that. I was a jerk to have spoiled that. Face it, we were both jerks.

"How did *your* summer work out?" Sonya asked stiffly.

"Pretty good. Phil was at Jayne's most of the time so it was almost like I had my own place." Actually, that sounds great, but if you don't have a girlfriend, all it is is lonely. (I'll explain about my parents and the complexities of their lives in a minute.)

"So, they're really serious?" Sonya has met Jayne a couple of times and really likes her. Sonya wants to be a shrink and Jayne has a something, master's, I think, in clinical psych, even though she's ended up doing physiotherapy at Bellevue.

"Yeah, I think maybe this is it—ta da! Well, Phil's thirty-six. He's not exactly a spring chicken."

Sonya shot me a scornful glance. "It's about time he grew up. All the others were little lobotomized stewardess-types. Jayne's a real *person*."

Danger zone. "True," I said guardedly.

"Maybe it's because he's almost forty," Sonya went on. "He really wants someone to talk to, not just a faceless blob."

"Right."

I was being so amazingly restrained that, of course, Sonya finally exploded. "What'd you do, have an operation on your vocal cords? 'Right,' 'true,' " she mimicked. "You don't even agree with me."

"No, I do agree. Seriously. I do. I think Jayne's the girl—oops, woman—for Phil. I think they'll even get married. I couldn't be happier for them."

The elevator door opened. "God, you're a shit," Sonya said disgustedly.

See what I get for being nice?

Since we live in an old creaky West Side building, the elevator takes hours to creep from floor to floor. People could start courtships in our elevator, die, have babies. There're few acts that you couldn't complete going from the lobby to eight (Sonya's floor) or twelve (Phil's floor, where I live most of the time). Usually the only signs up in the elevator are: EXTERMINATOR HERE TUESDAY. IF YOU WANT HIM, SINE PAPER, placed there by the Cuban super. Since Phil believes in boric acid for roaches, and I don't much care, we never "sine."

But this time there was a new sign: DOG WALKER WANTED. CALL MRS. BERNSTEIN, 864-0983. "Who's she?" I asked, trying to get back on Sonya's good side before we reached eight.

"How should I know? Maybe one of the new ones?"

Our landlord is trying to pitch out all the little old couples who are paying beans for rent, and substitute for them young yuppie couples who can afford anything he wants to charge. Phil has lived here fifteen years, ever since he and Penny, my mom, split up. Usually, even if you don't know faces or aren't on intimate relations with the other occupants of the building, you know them by name. But Bernstein didn't ring a bell. "They could be on the other side."

Sonya arched an eyebrow. "So, are you going to apply for the job?"

"I might. . . . Depends on what kind of dog."

We were at eight. "Good luck," Sonya said dryly. The elevator door shut.

I always wanted a dog. But Penny's allergic to them, and Phil says he won't get one until they invent a self-walking variety, so all we ever had, at either establishment, were the usual fish, gerbils, and a non-singing canary. I like big dogs, the kind that are hard to have in the city—Labradors, weimaraners, Old English sheepdogs.

Phil has a good deal with his apartment. Or should I say *our* apartment? If you tried to move into Manhattan now, with a job like Phil's—he's in marketing at a small graphic-design company in Brooklyn—you might, if you were lucky, get a broom closet over on Ninth Avenue and Forty-second

Street. But when Phil and Penny split up, his grandmother, who used to live in this building, died. So he got a great one-bedroom place in a decent neighborhood. There's even a dining room and, in the back, a little room known as a maid's room, where I hang out when I'm sleeping there.

Sonya says everything important that happens to form someone's character takes place before they reach the age of five. Given my origins, this probably gives me the right to be as neurotic as all get-out in the years to come. Flashback to the early seventies. Bronx Science. A big public high school in New York. Penny, then sixteen, and Phil, then seventeen, are, in the vernacular of the day, "going together." First love. They met in Physics Lab. Penny, who was pert and freckled and blonde, dropped things and always acted adorably out of it and Phil, who isn't a whiz at science but was good enough to get A's, helped her. She was cute and he was smart. That was how they both saw it then. The perfect couple except that Penny was Catholic and Phil was Jewish, but even that added some spice. Enraged parents, the lure of the exotic, and so forth.

Sex was "making out" which I gather included everything but the lurid act itself. Penny claims she wasn't a prude and had already broken away mentally from her Catholic up-bringing, but I guess not quite enough. Also, she says, she was scared. They didn't have a lot available in the way of birth control or, more important, birth-control information. Then Phil met Oscar Lombardo, a guy who worked with my grandfather. He claimed he had a perfect birth-control method for men. You just took a little pill once a week and you were sterile until you stopped taking it. Phil was nervous, but Lombardo swore *he'd* used it for years as a swinging bachelor, and had never gotten *anyone* knocked up. It seemed so easy! Only, like most things that seem easy, it didn't work. A month later—this was senior year for Phil, junior for Penny—Pen missed her period and then again and then again, and finally—as Lombardo finally admitted with a shrug, "Everything doesn't work some of the time."

That was how I was conceived. By two scared, nervous kids who, as Phil says, "didn't know up from down." Abortion wasn't an option, they were in love, Penny was coming to school with red eyes, up all night crying. Phil decided to "be a man." They were married secretly over spring vacation, but didn't tell either set of parents till Penny began to show. By then it was a kind of fait accompli. Ultimately both sides of the family simmered down. Phil's mother, my grandmother Rose, thought Penny had done it on purpose to ruin Phil's future. Penny's father, my grandfather Will, thought Phil had invented the Lombardo hoax in order to have sex with an innocent, sweet Catholic virgin. There's a photo of the two of them, not at their marriage which went unrecorded by film, but at Phil's high-school graduation. By then Penny was, shall we say, in full bloom, wearing a lacy white dress, her belly sticking out a mile. Phil is holding her hand tightly, trying to smile with bravado. He looks scared shitless.

Several years of teenage marriage, Phil working, going to college at night, Penny stuck home with a baby (me) who had a wandering eye and eczema and started talking back at nine months. Maybe another couple would have hung in there for a decade or even a century, but they decided, at the ages of twenty and twenty-two, to, as Phil now puts it, "cut their losses." His grandma died so Phil got the apartment. Penny moved back to her parents' house in Queens with me and started college. Her mother looked after me during the day. You could call it Joint Custody only the term hadn't been invented yet and, as both of them like to joke, the only thing they fought about in the divorce was who would have me. Penny wanted Phil to have me and Phil wanted Penny to have me. What ended *up* happening was I spent the next couple of years in Queens (in itself a debilitating experience even though I don't remember any of it). Then, when I was eight, Penny met Mike, married him and moved back into the city, to Riverdale, where they've lived happily and peacefully ever since with their two kids, Seth, who's seven and Susie, who's four. My step-sibs.

So I alternate. It's a better deal at Phil's but till I entered high school there was the flow of his girlfriends. Either they slept over (bad influence on me, according to Penny) or Phil slept at their places which meant I was alone. At Penny and

Mike's, the problem is there's no extra bedroom, now that the kids are born. I sleep in the living room, but it doesn't have a door and, as you can imagine, trying to study with two little kids coming in every second isn't the easiest. Since high school the problem of what would be good for me or bad for me seemed to go away, or maybe Phil and Penny were too much into their own lives to worry about it nonstop. I seem to have survived. "Maybe it's been good for you," Penny says. "Maybe it's made you more mature."

Maybe. The last word isn't in yet, but as Oscar Lombardo might have put it, time will tell.

CHAPTER 2

Now you know the basics of my family background, so whatever happens from here on, just keep all that in the back of your mind, if, like Sonya, you believe it makes any difference. If, like me, you don't—just pitch it.

I decided to check out the dog-walking job. My job at Books is only two days a week, ten to six on Tuesday, and one to ten in the evening on Friday. My days are pretty much open-ended. Even though I hadn't written down the Bernstein phone number, I remembered it. That's a quirk I've had since I was little. I can look at almost any number and it implants itself in my brain. Useless numbers, most of the time, but it can be helpful occasionally. I'll never forget a girl's phone number, should that situation ever present itself.

I went down to the lobby. Pablo was on duty. Ernando, our super, brought in all his relatives when he got the job eight years ago and they're pretty nice guys, even if their grasp of English ranges from shaky to nonexistent. "Hey Pablo," I said. "Do you know who Mrs. Bernstein is?"

"With the dog?" he asked.

"Yeah, right. . . . I saw that notice and I—"

"Seven-A," he said, "She in now. You go."

"Is it a nice dog?" I asked. "I mean, it's not ferocious or vicious or anything?"

Pablo laughed. "Little dog." He gestured. "Little *little* dog. You carry it in the palm of your hand. No ferocious."

I hope it's not a chihuahua. They always look like rats to me. Damn, I was hoping, if not for a Saint Bernard, at least for something middle-sized. I personally think mutts are the most intelligent dogs. Still, how can it hurt to check it out?

Seven-A is on the other side of the building. Unless you live in New York, you might not realize that the other side of the building is a whole other world. You might not even run into people who live on *your* side all that much, but the ones on the other side could be in Nebraska. They even have a separate elevator. The A apartments are the ones that are considered the most desirable. I know because for years Phil tried to get one and finally gave up. The difference in the A's is that you don't have to walk through the dining room to get to the kitchen so potentially the dining room can be another bedroom. That's it—but in New York people kill for one extra bedroom.

I rang the doorbell. A minute later I heard shrill yapping (as opposed to barking) and the door opened. A girl stood there—big, black eyes, a Mickey Mouse T-shirt, faded jeans, barefoot. She was about five feet tall, probably around my age or a year or two younger. A little scraggly Yorkshire terrier, my least favorite scraggly dog after chihuahuas, was leaping around. "Hi," the girl said. "Shh, Baby. Cut it out. . . . Are you here about the dog-walking?"

"Yeah, I . . . Is your mother home?"

She laughed. "My mother? Probably. Only she lives three hundred miles from here. Do you have a message for her?"

I turned red. Clearly, in a decade or so, I'll be so suave and urbane around women of all ages that I'll make Cary Grant look sick. But right now it comes and goes, mainly goes. "I—the sign said Mrs. Bernstein," I stammered.

"Yeah, that's me." She smiled, but not in an unkind way. "And that's Baby. I apologize for the idiot name. I got him when he was a baby and I never could think of a real name for him, so it sort of stuck. He's ancient now."

"How old?" What if he died while I was walking him? Would I need malpractice insurance?

"Fourteen." She bent down and scratched him affectionately behind the ears. "He has every malady known to man or beast. It's really sad. Like us, only it happens more quickly."

At first I wasn't sure who "us" was—her and me or just mankind in general. I assumed the latter. *She* looked perfectly healthy. I kept staring at *him*. God, what a wretched dog! As I've said, little yapping terriers aren't my favorite dogs, but this one had lost most of its hair and had some kind of horrible eczema on its rear end. I hope someone puts me to sleep when I start looking like that. "You haven't thought of, um, putting him to sleep?" I suggested tentatively.

The girl, Mrs. Bernstein, looked horrified. "Why? He's not in pain. I mean, if he was suffering . . ." Suddenly she looked belligerent. "Listen, do you love dogs? Because I only want someone who *loves* them. This isn't just a way for some kid to make extra money after school."

Kid! Thanks a lot, lady. "I do love dogs," I said. I hesitated. "I just thought . . . he'd be bigger."

"How can he be bigger? That's the size Yorkshire terriers are! The sign didn't say anything about his size."

I cleared my throat. "No, I just . . . It's just that my own favorite kinds of dogs are Labradors and weimaraners and—"

She flushed. "So find one of those! Look, I've had other people calling about this job. You're not doing me any favors by taking it."

I tried to look ingratiating, to get back on a good footing. "No, I'd like to, well, try it. . . . Let's see how we get along." I bent down and let Baby sniff my hand.

The girl watched approvingly. "That's good. You don't just go at him. So many people scare dogs by going straight at them. They don't realize they have feelings, just like people."

I hoped she wasn't the type that knitted him little booties

and scarves in the winter and called him by sickening pet names. "Baby" was bad enough. I vowed never to use it publicly, even when he was off the leash and about to be run down by a truck. I straightened up. "What would the hours be?"

"Monday, Wednesday, and Friday at four would be the best." She looked up at me. I wondered how old she'd been when she got married. Younger than Penny, probably. Maybe she was from the South. I've heard the laws are different down there. "See, I dropped out of college and now I'm going back and some of my classes meet in the late afternoon."

"That's sort of what my mother did," I said, still trying to be friendly.

She frowned. I noticed for the first time that she had a little heart drawn on her cheek. A tattoo? She was cute, I had to admit it, a lot cuter than her dog. "What do you mean?"

"No, I just meant—my mother met my father in high school and she dropped out—" I decided to leave out the pregnancy. "—but then she went back and finished up and now she's doing well. I mean, she likes what she's doing. She's a paralegal. She says those years off gave her time to think about what her real goals were."

Was I talking too much? Why was I talking about my mother? But Mrs. Bernstein said, "Well, I'm not . . . I finished high school. I was in college. I'm twenty-two. You thought I was younger, right?"

I hesitated. "Well, yeah."

She laughed. "People always do. I'm not insulted. I mean I *can* look older when I get all fixed up, but right now I'm just at home, so . . ." She looked up at me appraisingly. "How come you applied for the job?"

"I live in the building. . . . I mean my father does. Phil Gold. We're on the other side." That way, if she wanted to check my credentials, she could just ask Pablo or one of the other doormen.

"How come you don't live with your mother?"

"I do some of the time. . . . Only she's remarried and has two little kids. It's more peaceful here."

"Didn't your father remarry? I thought usually fathers do first."

"No, he just kind of . . . played the field. What I mean is," not wanting Phil to sound like a jerk, "he had girl-friends, but he didn't . . . I guess he wanted to take some time making up his mind. He figured he'd married too young the first time and he wanted it to really work the second time."

I was afraid, as I was in the middle of that sentence, that she'd take it as an insult, since she, obviously, had married pretty young too. But she just said quietly with a little sigh, "I guess you never know."

"I'm not getting married till I'm thirty-five," I said, drawing myself up, "if then."

Why was I telling her all this? We ought to be talking about dogs! "Why?" she asked.

"Well, I guess, partly because I want to be a playwright, and I think it takes at least that long to get established." I didn't add how having a string of intense, fascinating women would be more exciting than a wife asking what time I'd be home for dinner. Plus I figure I should know about women so I can put them in my plays. I admire playwrights like Pinter and David Hare who write good parts for women.

She looked really interested. "Do you write plays? I'm taking Modern Drama. That's one of my courses."

"Yeah, I—" I tried to weave a delicate balance between grandiosity and humility. "I've written *some* plays. They've put a few on at my school. Hamilton. I'm a senior in high school." I felt I had to admit that.

"And you've already written plays and had them put on? Boy, I'm really impressed. I never thought I'd get someone like you! Don't you need to spend your spare time writing?"

"I have a lot of spare time." For some reason, at that I blushed.

She was still gazing at me in admiration. "I'm *so* impressed by someone who can actually write a whole thing, a whole *anything*, with a beginning, middle and an end. That's

13

great. And you're just in high school. At your age, I knew nothing. *Less* than nothing."

I was beginning to really like her. I had a flash-image that her husband was in an irreversible coma and around eighty years old. "My name is Zoe," she said. "I just put 'Mrs. Bernstein' because I thought it sounded official."

"So, your husband is Jewish?"

"Yeah, so?"

"No, it's just—it's like my parents. Phil is Jewish and Penny is, was, Catholic."

"How come you call them by their first names?"

"I don't know. It just fell out that way, I guess. They never felt like parents, so they said, they were so young." I wondered if she had kids. The apartment was extremely quiet, but *it* or *they* could be asleep. Don't have kids, I begged her silently.

She was still gazing at me reflectively. "It's good to wait, I guess," she said in a slightly sad, plaintive way.

"Yeah." What do I know? What do I know about anything really? I just stood there.

Then Zoe reached out and shook my hand. Her hand was small and cool. "So, it's a deal? And maybe, well, my husband and I sometimes go away on weekends so if you could do it then, we'd pay extra."

"That sounds fine. I'm usually around on weekends." Shit. He clearly wasn't in a coma. Maybe a wheelchair? He could be a paraplegic from Vietnam who'd never fit into civilian life.

She reached to open the door behind me. "Did you mention your name?"

"Paul. . . . Here's my number. I'm right across the lobby so if you ever, if anything ever comes up, like you're sick or anything, or you need me to get some groceries, just give me a buzz, okay?"

I was afraid that was overdoing it, but she smiled. "That's really nice of you, Paul. I'm *so* glad you were the first one to come in person to answer the ad! I might've taken someone else."

God, what a nice girl—or is she a woman? What do you

14

call someone who's twenty-two and married but who looks like fifteen? Sonya says you can't call anyone over fourteen a girl, but I think you're allowed to call them girls till they're out of college. Zoe Bernstein isn't out of college yet. It's hard to think of someone like that as a "woman." She has nice breasts. Small, but nice.

I came back to our apartment to the sound of someone rattling around in the kitchen. It was Phil. He became a vegetarian about five years ago, but Jayne has convinced him it's okay to eat chicken and fish. I'm glad, because I was beginning to turn snarling and dyspeptic at the sight of a bean sprout. "I just got a job," I yelled.

Clearly, from my euphoric tone of voice, Phil thought it was something big. "Where? Tell me about it."

I pulled out a stool and watched him grate some ginger. He always puts ginger in fish. "No, it's just . . . I'm going to walk someone's dog. They live on the other side of the building."

"Oh, right. I saw the sign."

Part of me wanted to tell Phil the whole story, about Zoe Bernstein, how she'd looked young, but had turned out to be older, how impressed she'd been by my being a playwright, the cute way she'd had of looking up at me. Even that little heart on her cheek. It was corny and I usually hate girls who do that kind of thing, but on her it looked nice. Then I thought, seriously thought for the first time, of that dog. What was I getting into? So, Zoe Bernstein was cute? She wouldn't even be there when I walked him. She'd probably pay me by check. Leave it in the mailbox in the lobby. I suddenly felt horribly depressed. "It's a really ugly, ancient dog," I said despondently.

"So, why're you doing it?" Phil is a very open, good-natured person. There's never any double entendre or deep gnarled stuff going on with him. In fact—I know this is going to sound slightly obnoxious and condescending coming from an eighteen-year-old about his father—he's kind of a naive guy. Not *dumb* naive. You couldn't sell him the Brooklyn Bridge. Just not at all wily or complex. Like that Lombardo thing. You could say Phil was just a teenager at the time, but even at ten I wouldn't have fallen for a story like that. Phil is trusting. So, you could say why not discuss sex with Phil? I mean, there's no reason not to. He wouldn't lecture me one way or the other. He's had lots of girlfriends who haven't worked out, so he doesn't set himself forth as an expert. But the fact is, he doesn't even know I'm not a virgin anymore.

I don't *think* he does, anyway. It happened while he was at Jayne's.

"Where's Jayne?" I asked. Usually the three of us eat together.

"With Marsha, that dippy one who's getting divorced. I think she wants to cry on Jayne's shoulder."

Jayne has good shoulders for that. She's tall, a few inches taller than Phil, who's about five-nine. I'd call her attractive, rather than gorgeous or cute. She works out at a gym—that's how she met Phil who, though he's in better shape than he's ever been in, is not someone you'd pick for looks. In my opinion, anyway. He's mostly bald, except for little tufts on the sides of his head and when he goes jogging in his little red baseball hat, in his plaid shorts . . . well, like I say, he's a nice guy, and Jayne, who's in her thirties, probably hadn't met a lot of nice guys in New York.

Phil brought the shrimp and pea pods into the dining room. "So, how's school? Life? Sex?"

That was vague enough so I knew I could answer whatever part of it I wanted. "I just have two courses. College Lit and Psych. Life is life. And sex, well . . ." I shrugged sheepishly.

Phil sawed off a chunk of French bread. "Paulie, let me tell you something, straight from the shoulder. This is true now and it'll be true when you're my age and it'll be true when you're eighty. Half of what you hear from other guys is bullshit. Either they're not doing it or they're doing it and it's lousy. . . . What I'm saying is, don't feel you have to rush into things. Let it happen by itself. If you like a girl, it'll happen. In my day, no. It was marriage or nothing. But in your day—anything's possible."

I wonder if every generation has the illusion that the younger one has an easier, better time of it. Maybe people have to believe in progress, one way or the other. But I think Phil is right. What will be will be. I speared a pea pod. "You may be right," I said.

"I went through such stupidities with women . . . since I was *born*, practically," Phil said. "Proving this, proving that. Trying to rescue them, trying to make them happy. Forget all that. Forget *proving*. Enlightened self-interest. I'm not saying be a schmuck, understand."

Sonya. Help! Was I a schmuck with Sonya?

"How would you define 'schmuck'?" I asked.

Phil leaned back and roared. That's the way he laughs. "How would I *define* 'schmuck'? What is this? A TV quiz show? A guy who makes women cry, who says A and means B, who promises stuff and doesn't do it."

"Were you ever like that?"

Phil gave a wry shrug. "Well, listen, I was a bachelor, what, fifteen years. Sure, I was a little bit like that some of the time. But not all-out. Ask any of them and I bet half, no, three-quarters, would say, 'He was a good guy.' My record is pretty clean. Of course, I'm not running for office."

CHAPTER 3

After dinner I went to my room, and started to read *Mrs. Dalloway*, our first assignment for College Lit. But in my head was a private assignment. A short story. Title: *Was I a Schmuck with Sonya?*

I feel like I have to clear my record here or at least set it straight. It's not half as bad as what you're probably imagining. In fact, if I had come right out with it at the beginning, the issue wouldn't even have arisen. You'd just be thinking what a nice guy I am. I *am*! I'm a nice guy.

A short replay of me and Sonya. In seventh grade she was my Big Sib. They do that at Hamilton, have a kid who's been in the school a long time take one of the new kids under his or her wing, help them get settled in. Sonya was great at that. She's an only child. She never had a little brother, and maybe that's how I seemed to her—helpless, inept, but smart. We became friends.

A side note. I've always had friends who were girls. My best friend has usually been a guy, in fact always, but I never went through what Sonya calls the latency period where you're supposed to hate girls. I thought some girls were jerks the way I thought some guys were jerks. But there was always at least one girl I felt like I could talk to or who was interested in what I was interested in. But with Sonya it was more serious or more intense because we were older, almost teen-agers—some kids in our class were going out on dates at twelve—and also because we lived in the same building. We were both in the Chess Club; neither of us whizzes, but in-terested enough to follow major matches in the papers or on TV. Sonya was always more interested in the psychological aspect—why did certain players make certain moves, what did it show about their personality—but it was the only "sport" we both cared about. Then, later, in high school, came Playhouse 74. It's a special theater group in which Hamilton kids write, direct, cast, and act in their own plays. It's called Playhouse 74 because Hamilton used to be on Seventy-fourth Street. That's what I meant when I told Zoe Bernstein I'd had a play put on. Sure, it's not Broadway, it's not even Off *Off* Broadway, but some of the students are pretty decent actors and you do have an audience, scenery, the whole bit. Needless to say, the audience is almost entirely other kids in your class or parents or sibs, but still, it's inter-esting. Plus, they don't do everyone's plays. They only do three a semester. A lot more than that are handed in. The Committee, consisting of Sonya, me, my best friend Wolf, and a few others select the plays. I'd say it's fair. Both Wolf and Sonya would veto one of my plays if they didn't like it. What I mean is, they take it seriously enough so that even friendship doesn't get a play accepted automatically.

Some of the plays are hopeless, the ones you don't even have to read to reject. You just look at page one and know: forget it. Some are in-between: a good idea, only rambling; a derivative idea, only well-written. Only once or twice in the whole time I've been at Hamilton has there been a play about which I felt pure and total envy. My ambition is to write one like that this year, get it all together somehow.

Mostly Sonya and I hung out in a crowd of kids, going to parties, having classes at school. There were pairings-up from time to time, though nothing as uncool as "going together." Mainly—you may have picked up on this by now—I was the type who gazed from afar, decided it was hopeless, or would wait endlessly until whoever it was found someone else. Or there'd be things like the Kitty Berg incident. Kitty seemed to have some kind of crush on me. On Valentine's Day in ninth grade she sent me a white carnation, with some kind of cute little note. That's a custom at our school. Either sex can do it, but more boys do it than girls. I hadn't sent anyone a carnation. Anyway, by the time I finally got my act together with Kitty mentally, was convinced by Sonya, Wolf, and everyone that she genuinely liked me, she'd decided she was gay. Some women drive men to the bottle. I make women switch their sexual orientation.

So my social life till eleventh grade was nothing to write home about, even had I been away from home. But, I also never felt out of it or weird since the same was true of Sonya, Wolf, and most of our crowd. We joked, saying we were too cerebral to know how to do it, or our sexual energies were being drained by all the homework we got. But I'd say I was closer to being typical of a Hamilton junior than atypical.

Now we set the stage for "the fatal night." But first—this is more hindsight—I did notice in the spring of junior year that Sonya was acting a little more affectionate. Since it was always in her bantering, slightly hostile style, I never thought much of it. Maybe I'm slow on the uptake, but until that night I thought, to the extent I thought about it at all, that maybe Sonya was growing up a little, not being such a snot-nose kid, maybe learning to treat the male sex with some restraint. In short, I was enjoying her company more without plotting any moves. Sure, it had occurred to me that Sonya had gotten pretty. Wolf and I talked about that. Not beauty-queen pretty, but sometimes, at night, at parties, a certain luminous quality, bright eyes, that thick crinkly hair . . .

That particular night, Jayne, Phil, Sonya, and I ate out at a Greek restaurant in the Village. Sonya likes Jayne, and Phil and Jayne both like Sonya, so it was relaxed, not a "date"— we'd just been down there looking at an art show in Soho by one of Jayne's friends. At dinner Sonya got sloshed. She's not much of a drinker, but the owner of the restaurant knew Phil and kept bringing free bottles of a viciously strong Greek red wine. We all got a little high and silly. Phil began drawing cartoons on the paper mats, and Sonya joined him and everyone was laughing to excess over not especially funny things. I didn't even notice Sonya was sloshed until she got up to go to the ladies' room and was so unsteady on her feet that she knocked into the table and spilled her wine.

"Oh no," she said, "I think I may be drunk."

Jayne leaped to her feet and helped Sonya to the ladies' room, looking concerned. Phil looked at me and shrugged. "I guess she can't handle her liquor too well."

"I hope she's not going to be sick," I said.

"She'll be okay," Phil said in his reassuring way. "Let's order some black coffee." He hailed the waiter and told him to take away the unfinished bottle. "I think we've all had enough."

When Jayne and Sonya returned, Sonya looked pale, but okay. Jayne was terrific, like an older sister, affectionate, kindly. I was really relieved she had been there to handle it. "Greek wine is murder," Jayne said as they both sat down again.

"Like Hungarian," Phil said. "Did you ever have Egri Bikaver? Bull's Blood? That really knocks you for a loop."

"Are you okay?" I asked Sonya quietly, nervously.

She half-smiled. "Sure, no, I'm sorry. . . . Listen, everyone, I'm really sorry."

In our crowd very few kids drink hard liquor. It's usually just beer. I don't even like wine myself. We all sobered up on the Greek coffee which was like mud, but maybe did have some good sobering-up qualities. Sonya had gotten very quiet. She hardly spoke after the ladies'-room incident.

When we got out of the restaurant, it was raining lightly. Phil was going back to Jayne's for the night. She lives in Soho. "I'll get you a cab," Phil said to us.

I laughed. "I can get a cab," I said, "*I'm* not drunk." Then, realizing that was a little rude to Sonya, I said, "We're both fine."

Despite that, the four of us stood in the rain until a cab came. Phil ushered us in and even gave the cab driver our address. I didn't quite get why he did that since, as I say, I

21

was as sober as he was. In the cab Sonya just closed her eyes and slumped over, her head on my shoulder. I figured she was still woozy and I didn't think too much of it until she half-opened her eyes and said in a dreamy voice, "You have a funny, nice smell . . . like wine and violins and pine cones."

It was now maybe one in the morning. Mainly I felt very sleepy, not hung over but slightly glazed. What I said, without even thinking (it's the kind of remark you wouldn't make if you were capable of thought) was, "You too."

Then Sonya raised her head up just a little and said in that same sleepy voice, "Wouldn't it be weird if I was falling in love with you?"

If you've ever been even slightly drunk, you'll realize that a conversation that, in the light of day, you'd never get into in the first place, doesn't even seem strange. You'd think I'd have been amazed, delighted, horrified, but really I was too zonked to have any reaction that clear-cut. I just reached over and took her hand and, for the rest of the cab ride, we sat like that, Sonya's head on my shoulder, our fingers intertwined, our eyes closed. The cab driver had to tell us when we got to our apartment building. "Hey kids," he shouted. I think he was Greek too. "You're here. You're home!"

I paid and we got out of the cab. At all fateful moments in life, luck or chance plays a role. If everything had been the same that night, Sonya's getting sloshed, the dopey conversation about pine cones and violins—but she had lived in another apartment building, I could either have dropped her off or given her money and had the cab driver take her home. Even if she'd lived on the other side of the building, we would've maybe kissed in the lobby and gone home to our respective beds. But we had to take the same elevator up and when I reached out to press 8, Sonya's floor, she put her hand over mine and said with a smile, "Phil and Jayne aren't home. . . . And my parents are away for the weekend."

I don't even know if I answered that. It was, after all, a statement of fact, though, in retrospect, it was more than that, but I couldn't very well have said, "No, Phil and Jayne

22

are home," since we had just left them in the Village twenty minutes earlier.

We entered the apartment and Sonya, like a sleepwalker, walked straight into Phil's bedroom. She lay down, fully clothed, on his bed and before I even started thinking, was sound asleep. I stood there, looking at her, again too confused and feeling too many different things to have one plain simple reaction like, say (joy): Sonya wants to go to bed with me! or (horror): Sonya wants to go to bed with me! What I think I thought was: Sonya is still drunk, she's asleep, she has all her clothes on, there is nothing strange about this situation.

I went in to brush my teeth and it did occur to me that I could sleep in my own bed. But I didn't. What I did was take off my shoes and lie down, also fully dressed, next to Sonya and, like her, fell asleep in one second.

Aha! Jerry Falwell might say. Here we have the end result of what happens with permissive parents, broken homes, too much rock music: a potentially dangerous situation. Two fully developed, sexually aware teenagers lying side by side in one bed. He may have something. I'm trying to tell this literally as I remember it, and yet there are fuzzy patches that aren't totally clear. I'd say the next thing I remember was coming to, in the dark, still with my clothes on, making out with Sonya. I think we were both half-awake, half-aware of what was happening. But the darkness and the remains of the booze made it all a little unreal. We didn't speak, which, given Sonya's and my personalities, was unusual. Clothes began disappearing. Not all at once, but gradually, without effort. It was like one of those Disney movies I used to see as a child where in one scene the flower is tightly coiled, and in the next it's in full bloom. So at one point we had all our clothes on, and at another later point—I really don't know if this took hours or minutes—we had no clothes on. And then . . . well, if this was a forties movie, it would pan to the crashing surf. But then we were making love, only—and I don't know exactly how to describe this—I think we were both still pretending we weren't. What I mean is if I had been conscious of the thought: I am screwing Sonya, I might

23

well have lost consciousness. And maybe, though I'll never know, vice versa.

We did it and then, believe it or not, we fell right back to sleep. Came the dawn! I woke up and heard Sonya rattling around in Phil's bathroom. I became aware that I was unclad. I became aware that, according to Phil's digital clock, it was eleven-fourteen. I felt petrified. Why, you might ask? Because if there was an innocent victim in this story, it was clearly me, right? Sonya got drunk, Sonya leaned on my shoulder in the cab, Sonya refused to go home to her own apartment, Sonya walked into Phil's bedroom. This isn't to say that I wasn't a willing and even eager participant, but never in a million years would I have taken any of those first steps.

Think back to one of the most embarrassing awful moments of your life. Kindergarten, when you peed on the floor, or having some bully sock you in the stomach for no reason in recess, and knowing you were too scared to fight back, getting caught smoking at school and having the principal threaten to have you expelled. Whatever. Such a moment was the one when Sonya walked out of the bathroom, fully clad, and looked at me, as I lay craven, naked, under the sheet. "Should I make some coffee?" she said.

"Sure, I'd love some." She looked scared and nervous too which, in one way, made it easier and in many other ways harder.

Sonya made coffee. I showered and got dressed. She was sitting pensively in the kitchen, drinking her coffee when I walked in. "I guess we were both pretty drunk last night," she said, not looking at me.

For a second I had a wild hope that she didn't remember anything. I've read about that, people getting sloshed and asking the next morning, "How was I?" "Yeah, well, Greek wine . . ." I mumbled, pouring some coffee from Phil's coffee machine which even grinds the beans for you.

Silence. We both contemplated every object in the room. Nice cabinets. Attractive mugs. Peeling paint. Finally Sonya said, "Do you want to go on with it?"

"With—?"

"What happened."

My tongue felt huge and furry. "You mean be—"

"Yeah."

Maybe the next part was cruel. I thought of it at the time as truthful. I said, "I don't think I'm in love with you." I remembered what she'd said in the cab.

"Why not?" Sonya asked in her more typical belligerent style.

I tried to joke. "Maybe I'm too young." I'm six months younger than Sonya. I had turned seventeen in April.

"So, why did you do it?" Sonya asked in a trembling, angry voice.

"Last night, you mean?"

"No, the hundred other times we've made love!"

"I was carried away, I guess. My body was doing the thinking, the reacting . . ."

"That's called using someone," Sonya said, her eyes bleak. "It's not what you do with a friend."

"I know. . . . I was a jerk." I was praying total penitence would see me through.

"You could have said, 'Go home, go to your own place,' " Sonya pursued. "You let me come here. Why?"

Sonya was my friend. I felt rotten. But I also felt something wasn't totally fair. "Son, I was somewhat sloshed, I didn't . . . think. I just . . . And then you collapsed on the bed. I thought maybe we'd both just sleep it off."

"You could have slept in your own bed."

"True."

I could see the jury leaning forward, writing in their pads. "Why didn't you sleep in your own bed?" Sonya went on sarcastically, "Did you forget the way?"

There were so many things I could have said, but I was scared she would leap on all of them. "I'm sorry," I said, trying to smile sheepishly, sweetly, apologetically.

"I was a virgin till last night," Sonya said.

"Me too." I smiled, still trying to joke her into a better mood. "At least neither of us'll get AIDS."

Sonya stood up. "I don't give a shit about losing my virginity, I just feel like a goddamn fool for trusting you, for

thinking you'd act like a sensitive, decent human being."
With that she stomped out of the apartment.

So, what was I supposed to do? Crawl to the door, weep at her feet? I mean, Christ, I said I was sorry! I mean, really, looked at honestly, this could be called Date Rape only by the female. Not a frequent occurrence, but couldn't it? Sitting, cold sober, in the kitchen, I thought: yes, I could and should have not let Sonya come to Phil's apartment, I could and should have slept in my own bed. But deep down a little secret part of me felt glad I hadn't. Not just some macho crap of: finally I've been laid. But, well, it had been good, even though I wasn't fully conscious every second. But I *was* flattered that Sonya had chosen me. And also, I was sure that, given time to think it over, she'd see it the way I did and we'd go back to being friends.

No such luck. The next day at school: stony glances, total coldness. Same all week. Luckily we only had about three more weeks of school but even Wolf said, "Did something happen with you and Sonya?"

Wolf's like Phil in some ways. You can tell him anything and he'll listen and say something that will make you feel better. But I didn't want to tell him. Or anyone. I just felt rotten and finally, angry at Sonya for making such a fucking big deal out of it.

So, there you have it. *Was* I a schmuck with Sonya?

CHAPTER 4

Wolf's student job is helping his Dad who does lung transplants at Memorial Hospital. He studies the tissue under the microscope. He wants to be a doctor. No David's Cookies stuff for him. But he only does it weekends so Monday, after school, he asked if I felt like coming over to his apartment. He'd been away over the summer on a bike trip in New England so we hadn't talked much since July. Neither of us ever write letters. Sonya doesn't really get my friendship with Wolf. We've know each other since we were three and we haven't always gone to the same school. There've been months, even years, when we haven't seen each other at all. Like I say, we don't write letters, we don't gab on the phone, but I know, when I'm fifty-five and having some stupid mid-life crisis, I'll call Wolf, wherever he is, and we'll talk and he'll understand. He's little and skinny with red hair and freckles, and he got an almost perfect score on his SATs. But he never boasts about that. I only know because some other kid at Hamilton found out and told everyone.

"Yeah, I'd love to," I said. "I—" Then I remembered

Zoe Bernstein. Monday at four. "Shit, I can't. I have this job."

"At the bookstore? I thought that was Tuesday and Friday."

"No, I'm just . . . I'm walking some lady's dog in our building."

"Every day?"

"Pretty much."

"Wouldn't that be a drag once Playhouse 74 gets started?"

I hadn't really thought of that. "I'm not even sure I'll do it for that long. I may rearrange the hours."

The more I thought of it as I walked home, the more I thought Wolf was right. To screw up three weekday afternoons for a mangy decrepit dog? Maybe he'd died over the weekend! Baby! For my first time Zoe Bernstein had said she'd be there, give me a key, and walk Baby with me so I could get the idea of his routine. In the back of my mind I toyed with telling her I'd changed my mind. She'd said she had a list of other people applying for the job. Face it—it was really a little kid's job.

When she opened the door, she looked different. I remembered what she'd said about looking older when she got dressed up. She wasn't all *that* dressed up, but she was wearing a red suit and high heels and her hair looked fluffed up in some way. She looked delighted to see me. "Hi. . . . Gosh, isn't it a great day?"

Phil is like that. You'll be taking a walk with him and he'll look up and say, "God, *look* at that sky!" Or you come in in the morning and he'll say, "Boy, did I sleep well! How about you?" To me a sky is a sky, something that covers the upper part of the atmosphere, that can be blue to gray. Maybe it's being a native city-dweller or just an insensitive cluck, but I don't get that excited about weather. And I figure when you're asleep, you're asleep; then you're up. But to Zoe Bernstein, I said, "Yeah, it's beautiful."

She got out Baby's leash and showed me how to clip it on. "The main thing is, never yank on the leash," she said, "because he's so delicate, like I said. The skin around his neck especially."

28

We left the apartment and waited for the elevator. "I always wanted a dog," I said. I was both trying to be ingratiating and also trying to let her know why I'd applied for the job.

"Why didn't you get one?" she said.

I explained about my parents. "In the city it's more of a big deal."

She looked understanding. "Yeah, when I got Baby, we were living in the country and I could just let him loose. We'd take these long walks together. Then, when I was thirteen, we moved into Philadelphia, and it was more like you say. . . . But I love him."

"Will you get another dog if he dies?" I hoped that wasn't a morbid question.

She looked sad. "I guess I don't like to think of it. My husband, he's like you, very practical, says just get another dog. But that's a little like saying get another boyfriend or another husband or another anything. What I mean is, Baby and I go back so far. He's, like, part of my childhood. . . . And then I'm back at school so it *is* more complicated." She smiled ruefully. "I don't really know."

"Maybe he'll live forever," I suggested.

I thought she'd get mad—it was a pretty stupid remark. But she looked pleased. "He could live another five years. Dogs do."

I wouldn't count on it, I thought. We passed through the lobby. Pablo saw us and winked. "No ferocious," he said, smiling. "Little dog, right?"

"Right." I felt embarrassed.

She looked up at me. "I'm sorry he's not a Labrador if that would've made you happier, but I hate big dogs myself. My brother used to have two German shepherds and they'd bring home animals they'd killed during the day. For no reason! I mean, they were fed extremely well. They'd bring home entire lambs! And just lay them on the doormat! I *hated* them!"

"That does sound pretty bad." Even if Baby were ferocious, I couldn't see him eating anything bigger than a gerbil. I looked around. Zoe was right. It was a gorgeous day—slightly warm, but not sticky, which is rare for New York.

"Do you want me to walk him on the park side or this side?" Our building is on Central Park West. There's a walk with trees across the street.

"I think the park side," Zoe said, glancing at it. "He loves grass and trees. Maybe because he grew up in the country. . . . Only never cross except when the light turns to 'Walk' because he goes so slowly. You might not make it."

"I could pick him up and carry him if we ever get stuck in the middle," I suggested.

"Yeah. . . . Only he doesn't like that so much. But if it's an emergency . . ."

When we got to the park side, she gave me the leash. "I want him to see that you're my friend. Not that he's paranoid, but he can be suspicious until he gets to know someone by smell. When I started dating Paul, Baby would really almost attack him. He bit him once."

"*My* name is Paul," I said, blushing.

"Oh, right, I know. . . . No, I meant my *husband* Paul. You know, it's strange—you probably won't even believe this, but my brother's name is Paul too. I was even going to name Baby 'Paul' when I first got him because it's one of my favorite names." She laughed. "I guess wherever I go people named Paul show up! It's not that I'm superstitious, but when you said your name was Paul, I knew it would work out."

Her husband. Maybe he looks exactly like me. Maybe he has my personality too. Maybe he is me. We are really a pair of identical twins, separated at birth and . . . "What does your husband do for a living?" I asked. Baby was sniffing around a tree.

"He has his own business. They make orthopedic shoes. Only they're attractive. They're not just for people with bad feet. They're really comfortable. He's an excellent businessman. He and his partner opened their fourth store last year. It's doing very well."

God, how creepy! Orthopedic shoes! Why would someone as nice and pretty as Zoe marry a guy who made orthopedic shoes? "Is he older than you?"

"Twelve years. He's thirty-four. Does that seem a lot older?" She looked like she really wanted my opinion.

Mike is eight years older than Penny. Jayne is five years younger than Phil. I guess it's pretty standard. The guy has made it, has lots of dough, he's fooled around a lot, is ready to settle down and have kids. But I was disappointed. I guess I wanted her to say he was her age and a would-be carpenter. Why would that be better? They couldn't afford to live in our building if that were true. I began forming a mental image of him: not too tall, dark, clean-cut, handsome features, one of those guys with a very firm handshake, maybe a Republican, decisive, dynamic, collects CDs. He sounded terrible. "I guess it's not so much age that matters," I said diplomatically.

Zoe looked pleased at that. "*I* think that," she said. "Some people are mature for their age, others never are. . . . I mean, I think it *was* a little the opposites-attract thing. Like to Paul, I seemed kind of this kooky, intense, artistic type and to me *he* seemed more settled and sure of himself than most college guys. He wasn't, like, lunging at me right from the first date."

A few flash-images of half-clad Zoe, struggling in sexual encounters in the backseats of cars, superimposed themselves on the sight of Baby squatting to take a shit. Suddenly I noticed that the little heart that had been on her cheek was gone. "You washed off the heart." I said. "I thought maybe it was a tattoo."

Zoe touched her cheek. She had soft, lovely skin, now lightly flushed. "I'm not *that* bad. A tattoo! No, that's what I mean, though. I am a little—I do have artistic leanings, I like to draw, I'm taking this short-story writing course, but I'm not . . . I'm not like you. I don't have inner drive. I'm more the type who does a bit of this and a bit of that, who starts things and then—"

Why was she so sure I had inner drive? "I've only written three plays," I said. "I start lots of things and don't finish them. I want to be a playwright, but I doubt I'll make it. A million people want to be playwrights."

Zoe stared at me with her big, black eyes. They were made up a little which made them look bigger. "No, you'll make it. I can tell. You *do* have inner drive. So does Paul, my husband Paul, I mean. That's why his stores are so successful. Lots of people make orthopedic shoes too. In fact, he was told not to do it because this other company seemed to have a monopoly on the market, but he thought of a better way.''

Was I supposed to be flattered or insulted? First, to be mercilessly accurate, I think there's a lot more competition if you want to be a successful playwright than if you want to sell orthopedic shoes. Not that I could run or start a company that sold orthopedic shoes or anything else, for that matter, but equating the two seemed a bit grotesque. On the other hand, looked at less closely, it was a compliment. She was saying she thought I'd make it. Not a lot of people have thought that, or, if they have, they've never voiced the opinion. ''Thanks,'' I said.

We crossed the street and headed back to the building. She bent down and scooped Baby up in her arms. She kissed him. ''Now you know Paul, right? He's a nice person who lives right in our building and he's always wanted a dog.''

This should have been the kind of thing that would turn my stomach totally, a woman talking in an intimate purring tone to a small eczema-ridden dog. But Zoe Bernstein looked so sweet and adorable in her red suit, the way she held Baby was so tender and affectionate, the way she peered up at me was so trusting and slightly embarrassed, like she knew she looked silly, that I was a dead duck. I would have walked the wretched dog for free at four A.M.

She gave me the key. ''Sometimes I might be home or sometimes not, but why don't we just say at four you'll walk him? I might be studying or napping, whatever. Just open the door, walk him, and then bring him back.''

Did that mean I'd never see her? I stood there, dismayed. ''Great,'' I said heartily, putting the key in my pocket. I walked disconsolately to the elevator. Why couldn't we walk him together every time? Because then there wouldn't be any point, fool! She wants you to walk him because she won't always be there.

Orthopedic shoes! Suddenly the day seemed not bright and beautiful, but dark and incomprehensible. Why was Zoe Bernstein so desperate? So the guy had money (maybe)? Why couldn't she marry some guy who was struggling, but whom she believed in, whom she knew, with her support, would someday make it? Sonya would hate this marriage. It really sounded sexist. He makes money, she futzes around, does "a bit of this and a bit of that." Is that all Zoe Bernstein wants out of life?

I was thinking of this when I had dinner at Penny and Mike's that night. It's hard to have a real conversation at dinner because Seth and Susie are usually screaming or spilling things. Mike is a pretty quiet guy anyway. He's tall and husky with curly black hair. He and Penny look so much alike they could be brother and sister. Since their marriage, Penny's put on a bit of weight, but so has he. They both look solid. Penny's the kind of person who should've been a nurse. All the chaos with the kids never seems to faze her. She drinks beer out of a can, like Mike, and they hug each other a lot. They don't have the kind of marriage I'd like to have, if I ever do marry. Intellectual communication is not high on their list of important priorities. Probably they fuck a lot. They never read. They don't even read the newspaper! They watch the evening news and if some movie star dies, Pen gets all upset. Mike goes into a lather if the Mets don't do well. That's it. I'm not saying they're Neanderthals. They're "just folks" and I like both of them. What are Paul and Zoe Bernstein like at home?

Susie tried to sit in my lap while we were having dessert, chocolate pudding with Dream Whip. Pen is not a gourmet cook. Susie's cute but, like me at that age, she's slightly cross-eyed. I hope they fix it. It looks weirder on a little girl, even, than on a boy. She likes feeding me. I let her.

"Susie, let Paul eat his own dessert," Penny said indulgently.

"It's okay," I said.

"Someone has a c-r-u-s-h on you in a *big* way," Penny said. "Every night we tell 'Paul stories.' You slay dragons, you rescue beautiful maidens—"

"All in a day's work," I said, opening my mouth and swallowing the last spoonful of the pudding.

"Boy, how do you stay so thin?" Mike said admiringly.

"Look at him! Not an ounce of fat." He patted his own beer belly affectionately.

"He probably works out," Penny said.

"I think it's just that I'm growing," I said.

"You look good," Mike said. "Don't you think he looks handsome, Susie?"

Susie looked up at me and then rolled her eyes and pretended to faint.

"I wish girls my age did that," I said. Susie leaped off my lap and she and Seth rushed off to watch TV.

"Don't worry," Mike said, "they will. Any day now." He burped. "Sorry."

Penny leaned forward and dipped her finger in the Dream Whip. "How about that little girl who used to baby-sit with you sometimes? The one with the frizzy blonde hair?"

I felt over-full. "Sonya?"

"Right. . . . I always had the feeling she liked you. Didn't you, Mike?"

"I can't remember that well," Mike admitted.

I certainly wasn't going to tell them about "my night with Sonya." "She's . . . I don't think we're that well-suited," I said.

"When I was your age, senior year of high school," Mike said, "did I have a cute girlfriend! Little, with big blue eyes and freckles. She looked sort of like you, Pen." He sighed. "I wonder what happened to her. Maureen O'Duffy."

Penny narrowed her eyes. "She's probably gained eighty pounds and is a lush with thirteen kids."

"Probably," Mike said amiably. He stood up and stretched. "Maybe I should go to our high-school reunion and see how she's turned out."

"If you do, I'm coming," Penny said, mock-threateningly. She got up to clear the table.

Mike slumped down in "his" chair, a comfortable plaid recliner. Sonya, need I even say, thought Mike and Penny's marriage was the ultimate in, as she put it, "sexist grossness." It's true, Penny always makes dinner and does the dishes, while Mike watches sports on TV. But, like I say, they love each other and they're happy, so why is that so bad?

He doesn't sock her or anything. He seems good with the kids.

Mike was still gazing dreamily off in the distance. "Maureen O'Duffy," he repeated. "You know what it was? I'll tell you. She was cute, sure, but she made me feel like a king. Whatever I did. It was real. She just fucking worshipped the ground I walked on."

"She sounds like a jerk," Penny yelled from the kitchen.

Mike winked at me. "How many people make you feel like a king, ever, then or now?"

"Not a lot," I said. In fact, more honestly, none in my case.

"She'd sit on my lap and lean her head on my shoulder . . ." He trailed off.

I sat there, thinking of Zoe Bernstein. Does she do that? Does she make her husband feel like a king? Doe she sit on his lap? I had this sudden image of her, naked, sitting on his lap. He was fully dressed and she was holding Baby on *her* lap.

Penny walked into the room. "Are you okay, Paul? You look a little funny."

The image vanished. "Sure, I'm fine. I was just thinking . . . Do you think it's good when the husband is older than the wife, I mean like with you and Mike?"

Penny shrugged. "I don't know. I don't think it matters that much. Do you, hon?"

Mike was, by now, riveted on the baseball game. "Huh?"

"Paul wants to know if we think the husband should be older than the wife for them to be happy and all?"

"Maybe a little older," Mike said, watching the game. "A couple of years."

"Why, though?" I persisted. "Why does it matter at all?"

Penny seemed puzzled by my intensity. "Well, I don't know. Maybe so he can be more established. Like, if she wants to have kids, he can give them a good home and things like that."

Suddenly I was furious. "So, he's rich? What if he's mean? I mean if they're both poor and the same age but happy, why shouldn't that work?"

"I guess it could," Penny said mildly. "It didn't for me, that's all. Why, are you thinking of getting married?" She smiled indulgently.

"No!" I yelled. What a jerk I am.

"The kid hasn't even lost his cherry yet. Why're you marrying him off?" Mike said.

I glared at him. Sometimes Mike can really be crude. Penny's my mother, after all. What could I say? *Yes, I have. I'll send the video over tomorrow morning.*

Penny must've sensed my irritation. She said, "We don't know all the details of Paul's sex life. . . . And no one's marrying him off. Susie would be heartbroken."

Before I left I went into the room the kids share and read them *I Had Trouble in Getting to Solla Solew* which is one of their and my favorite Dr. Seuss books. The hero never does get to Solla Solew. In fact, he just ends up going back home where you know things are pretty rotten. It's a fairly grim story for little kids, but they love it anyway. Maybe they don't see its existential implications yet.

I always take the A train home. Yes, I know the subway is full of rapists, perverts, and graffiti artists, but I'm not rich enough to take a cab or in good enough shape to walk. I just want to correct one possible misimpression you may have gotten when I jocularly gave you my family history. I don't know if it had overtones of "poor, neglected child of divorced parents." Actually, it was quite unlike that. Many of my friends' parents have gotten divorced, usually when they (my friends) were anywhere from ten to eighteen. That's harder, I think, because by then, even at the younger end of the spectrum, you've been around them long enough to perceive them as a couple and to expect them to stay together forever. It's funny—despite all the odds and statistics, I think most kids still think their parents will not get divorced.

The difference with me was that it all happened when I was so young, I never thought of Penny and Phil as a couple. I don't even remember those years when Pen and I were living in Queens with Grandma Rose. I mean, I have the odd flash-memory of me in a swing or of digging in the garden with my grandmother. But the earliest set of steady memories

I have date from when Pen and Mike were married and Phil had his present apartment. Also, neither of them have ever seemed that bitter about the marriage or me or having their early lives wrecked. Maybe that's not their character, or maybe they each found other lives early on. Penny is so easygoing, I can almost imagine her being happy married to any one of a bunch of guys. I think she likes kids and a fairly humdrum low-key life, and that's what she got. I can even see her being happy with Phil if, maybe, they'd met later. Though, it's true, Phil's girlfriends have been a little more high-powered than Pen, better jobs, more strong-minded, nothing like Sonya, but, if anything, he's picked women I thought were a little over his head.

The worst thing Pen used to say about Phil, in his days of revolving-door girlfriends was, "When is he going to grow up and settle down and make some decent girl happy?" But you'll notice how she put it that way, like she thought Phil had the capacity to make someone happy, even if it hadn't worked with her. Re Pen, Phil will say he thinks she's gone to seed a little, put on too much weight, that Mike is "not exactly an intellectual giant, I mean, face it, Einstein isn't trembling in his grave." Not that I think Einstein trembles in his grave when Phil opens his mouth either, but it's true, Phil does read, mainly idiot thrillers and self-help books, but his mind is capable of taking in a page of disyllabic words without turning to mush.

What would I want in a marriage or even a relationship? I don't know, but I know I haven't seen it yet, even from afar.

CHAPTER 5

We had our first Playhouse 74 meeting today. Sonya's mother has a Xerox machine in her office so Sonya usually Xeroxes a bunch of copies of whatever's handed in and then we all read them and discuss what we think.

"Are you doing one this year, Paul?" Annice Evans asked. She's a junior and a hair's-breadth short of attractive.

"Yeah, I'm working on one," I said.

"When will it be finished?" Sonya said in that flat, angry tone which she's used with me since the fateful night last May.

"It *is* finished, basically," I said. I always feel everyone can sense Sonya's hostility to me, but maybe it's just in my mind. "I'm just adding a few touches here and there."

Sonya drummed her fingers on the tabletop. "Well, can you get it to us by Friday? Because we can't have any special rules for people, just because we know them."

"I'll get it in by Friday," I said.

Wolf smiled. "Sherman Lersh sent one in. I haven't had a chance to look at it yet."

Last year there was a flap because Sherman Lersh wrote

a surrealist play in which everyone was supposed to throw green Jell-O at each other in the climactic scene. Our faculty advisor, Mr. Mason, threatened to quit. He helps us out as a favor. He's really an English teacher and doesn't get paid extra: basically he's a good guy. He's a smallish guy who wears odd hats, even indoors, maybe to conceal the fact that he's totally bald.

"I think Maria's is beautiful," Sonya said. "It's very moving."

Maria Cantor is in our class, but she mainly writes poetry. "Is it in verse?" Wolf asked.

"In a way, but not so that you notice it," Sonya said. "It's extremely original."

"What's yours about, Paul?" Annice asked in a friendly way.

I looked all around the room, hoping for a rabbit's hole into which I might escape. "It's about, um, friendship, basically."

"Between men and women or between people of the same sex?" she pursued, still in a friendly, un-Sonya-like way.

I cleared my throat. "I guess I'd rather have it stand on its own merits or lack of them," I said. "I'll have a copy to you by the end of the week."

"Friendship is a good topic," Wolf said. "Does it have crazy parents?"

Last year all the plays had crazy parents in them, and so some parents protested, not just the ones being portrayed, but the parent body in general. We promised to pull in our horns a little this time.

I left the meeting feeling uneasy. Will I be dead by Friday? Have I done something unspeakable in this play? It's really a description of that evening I mentioned with Sonya. Naturally, I've changed our characters completely, but I really wanted to show what sex is like, what it's *really* like, among kids our age. So much is sensationalist crap, like in the movies, just horny guys trying to make it with birdbrains. I thought if I took two basically intelligent, nice kids like Sonya and me, but showed how it's still a mess, despite the fact that everyone thinks that our generation has it easy. It's not *like* that! It's still painful and complicated. That's what I wanted to show. I think I'm going to call it *Just Friends*, but I'm not sure. I'm not great on titles. Sometimes Wolf helps me out.

I dropped my school bag at home, had a Coke and a whole wheat bagel, and set off to walk Baby. The Bernstein apartment was silent, but Baby, who by now seems to recognize me, came creeping out from the basket where he usually sleeps. I fastened his leash on and we set off. It was a gray day, cooler than the one when Zoe had gone on the walk with me, but Baby and I have our little routine: down to the corner, across the street. He circles around a particular tree and then seems to like to continue on down about half a block. Watching him, I can kind of see his mind going back and forth. I think Zoe's right: he likes grass and the feeling of being in the country and in the beginning he feels a little the way he must have felt when he was a puppy. And then somewhere between the first tree and halfway down the block, it must occur to him that moving around is a lot harder than it used to be. Once or twice, he just looks up at me with an expression that seems to say: boy, this is the pits. I can't even make it to the next tree! "Want me to carry you back?" I'll ask him. Usually he doesn't want me to. I know because when I bend down to try it, he backs away, as though I'd offended his doggy dignity. Or maybe he feels differently when Zoe does it. I would too.

Anyway, just as I had crossed to the park side I suddenly heard someone call, "Kid! Hey kid!" I wasn't aware that it was me who was being addressed. Actually I was thinking of the play, whether "Just Friends" was kind of a banal title, when a guy tapped me on the shoulder. He was tall and stout and had thick, slightly gray hair, and glasses. He was out of breath. "I'm Paul Bernstein. Just wanted to say hi. Zoe says you're doing a great job with the beast."

Jesus. This was not the Paul Bernstein whose image I'd been carrying around in my mind for the past five weeks. No way could you call him handsome or suave or forceful. Not ugly, not wimpish, but . . . dull. A clod. I wasn't jealous, just bewildered. "Hi," I said. "I'm Paul Gold."

We shook hands. He looked, I hate to be nasty, like someone who would run a chain of successful orthopedic-shoe stores. Zoe! *Why?* "I always wonder if he's going to last another day," Paul Bernstein said. "Look at him. All skin and bones. Isn't he ugly? How can Zoe love an animal like that?"

How can she love *you*? I wanted to say. "I guess because it was her first dog," I suggested.

Paul Bernstein sighed. "Maybe it's a child substitute," he said. "That's what my mother says. Women need something to love, something small and helpless."

So, why don't you get her pregnant, you jackass? I thought. No, don't get her pregnant, don't! "I like dogs," I said.

"Yeah, they're okay. . . . In the city it's a drag. You come home late at night, it's freezing cold and you stand there for hours, waiting for him to go. Or you want to go away on the weekend and . . . Hey, Zoe says you'd be willing to take him for a whole weekend. That'd be swell. We may take you up on that someday soon."

"I'd be glad to," I said.

He crossed the street and Baby and I continued our walk. Look, what the fuck difference does it matter *who* she's married to? Would you feel better if he looked like Mel Gibson? Yeah, in a weird way, maybe. This just doesn't make *sense*. Opposites attract. He makes money. He's calm, forceful. She didn't know any better. He didn't lunge at her. God, is *that* what women want? I don't believe it. Maybe she was pregnant, like Pen was, had an abortion, only by then it was too late . . .

A few weeks later in the middle of October, I ran into Paul Bernstein again. Though I hadn't seen Zoe much, I thought of her a lot, whether I was walking Baby or not. I had walked Baby and returned to the lobby. At Seven-A, the Bernsteins' apartment, I unlocked the door and then, I really don't know why, I called out, "I'm home! Baby's back!" I waited just a second. I thought maybe Zoe might be home. I hadn't seen her in a while and she could've come home since I'd left to walk Baby. No answer so I turned to go when suddenly Paul Bernstein, wearing a blue terrycloth bathrobe, came charging out of the other part of the house. "What's *wrong* with you? What're you yelling about?"

I looked around nervously. "I just—I thought, I—"

He grabbed me by the shoulder. "Look, kid, we pay you to walk the dog because we lead busy lives, right? So you walk him. You have your key, you walk the dog, and you let yourself out. That's all. Simple, right?"

"Right." My knees were shaking.

He straightened up and looked me right in the eye. "My wife was taking a *nap*," he said meaningfully.

I felt like someone had socked me right in the gut. Translation: we were fucking and right in the middle, right as she . . . you teenage incompetent, you wrecked it. I didn't come, she didn't come. You *wrecked* it. . . . I tried to look Paul Bernstein in the eye: Good, I'm glad. I hope you don't have another erection till the third appearance of Halley's comet. I slunk out of the apartment, my hand clenched around the key. My hands were sweaty, my heart beating ferociously. In my mind I went back, broke down the door, socked Paul Bernstein unconscious, flung him out the window, and made passionate love to grateful, adoring, delicate Zoe who was still lying sleepily, nakedly, in bed.

When I came back to our apartment, Jayne was there. She has Aerobics class every day after work. She looked radiant and muscular, in a feminine way. Jayne isn't my type, but I like her. Like I've said, I would have thought she could do better than Phil, which doesn't mean I don't think Phil is a great guy, but Jayne is smart, ambitious, clever. Opposites attract again? Does that mean I'll end up with a tiny woman with a brain the size of a pea who reads comic books and paints her toenails purple?

"I hate my job!" I yelled when I saw her.

She laughed. "That's *my* line. What job? The bookstore? I thought you loved it. Did they fire you? Did you have a fight with your boss?"

"My other job. I walk this lady's dog. She lives on the other side of our building."

"Oh, right, Phil told me." She was in a bathrobe, "Hey

Paul, is a vegetable curry okay for supper? I had to take some clients out to a steak house for lunch.''

''Whatever,'' I said morosely, taking off my jacket.

Jayne walked over and looked at me with concern. ''Hey, you really sound depressed. What happened?''

Nothing had happened. Nothing I could talk about, really. In a way Jayne is like a big sister, something I've never had—friendly, straightforward. I just shrugged.

''Come on in and have a beer while I do the curry. You can help me chop veggies.''

I sat on a stool. I was appalled at how lousy I felt. It seemed so totally out of proportion. What was it? Knowing Zoe Bernstein was in the sack with her lawfully wedded husband? His humiliating me? My acting like such a wimp? If I'd talked back, he'd have fired me. I chopped celery and sipped the beer which tasted wonderful.

''Is it something to do with a girl?'' Jayne asked. She was chopping carrots.

''Indirectly.''

''Someone you like who doesn't know you like her?''

''In a sense.''

Feminine intuition makes me nervous. I was sure in one second she would have the whole thing figured out. I kind of wanted her to, but basically I didn't. ''That can be shit,'' Jayne said. ''I had this massive crush on a guy in my Genetics class freshman year and he didn't, really, know who I was. I guess I was too tall or too something. Or maybe our hormones didn't mesh.''

I was staring at her with a mournful, paralyzed expression. ''She's going with another guy,'' I said. I decided to substitute ''going with'' for ''married to.'' ''And he seems like such a fool! And mean, even.''

''To her?'' Jayne looked alarmed.

''No, I guess he's okay to *her*. I wouldn't really know. I don't even know her that well.''

Jayne smiled at me in the nicest possible way. ''I think after three seconds you know everything about a person. I really do. Does that make me sound like a hopeless romantic? Like with Phil, it all grew and got more solid and richer, but I remember after the first five seconds, thinking, 'What a *nice* guy' in a way I hadn't for, maybe ten years."

What had Zoe been thinking when her husband had charged out of the bedroom? Maybe she had yelled at him when he came back? I imagined her furious. *How could you act so stupidly to Paul? Call up and apologize immediately!* "She's a little bit older than me," I said, shoving the celery to one side. "Not a lot. Just a little."

"Oh, that doesn't matter anymore. My brother just married a woman ten years older than him and they couldn't be happier."

"Really?" That was the first piece of good news I'd heard all day. Suddenly I felt very interested in Jayne's family. "How, uh, old are they?"

"He's about twenty-eight and she's about thirty-eight. She was married before. But, like I said, they're as happy as clams. And the woman he went with before this was fifteen years older so Mom and Dad aren't as hysterical as they might be."

"You don't think it's sort of sick or Oedipal?" I pursued. "I mean, no offense to your mother, but, like, he wants to be mothered or—"

"What guy doesn't? No, frankly, if you want to be psychological about it, I think Mom was terrific and I was a terrific older sister and it all makes perfect sense."

I leaped up and hugged Jayne. "I love you."

Jayne blushed. "Thanks, Paul. . . . I always wondered . . . Well, I never wanted you to feel I was overdoing the potential stepmother bit, but I'm glad. I love you too."

It's so simple when "love" is something within such wonderfully circumscribed limits. I felt good, too, though, whether just from hearing about Jayne's brother or from her commonsensical advice. In fact, another cheering thought occurred to me as I helped pass Jayne the spices. What if they hadn't been making love at all? *Retrace the steps.* I call out. Paul B. emerges, angry, in a blue bathrobe and says, "My wife was taking a nap." Maybe that's all she was doing! Maybe she's even been sick, a flu, something, and that's why he came home early from work. So, of course, he was upset, with a sick wife on his hands. . . . Then what was he doing in his bathrobe? He decided to take a nap too! People *do* nap. Especially in middle age. He's only thirty-four. Still, his hair is gray, he's exhausted from the stress of running all these stores. Probably they don't even *have* a sex life. They were just lying peacefully, side by side, he was snoring, his mouth open like my Uncle Harry does, Zoe was dreaming peacefully of . . . me?

I didn't really accept that fantasy, but I didn't dismiss it either. If you have a choice between two possibilities, why not choose the one that makes you feel better, right? The one thing I did was to call the Bernstein number from school the next day.

"Oh hi, uh, Zoe? This is Paul Gold, I just thought I'd check with you. Your husband mentioned you might be going away some weekend soon and I wondered if you knew exactly when it might be."

"Oh, of course. That was really inconsiderate of me," Zoe said. She sneezed. Hey, maybe she did have a cold! "I think it'll be the weekend after next, November eighteenth. Would that be okay?"

"Sure, that'd be fine,"

"Next time you walk Baby, we can talk about it. I've been feeling a little under the weather. I think I'll cut class today."

"I'm really sorry to hear that." Yay! Hurray!

"It's nothing serious, just a flu. You know the kind where you wake up feeling like you'd been run over by a Mack truck?"

I hesitated. "Listen, what I also called about was I'm extremely sorry that I woke you up from your nap yesterday, yelling out like that. It was just totally stupid."

Zoe hesitated a little too. "That's okay, Paul, really. I wasn't exactly asleep. . . ."

I waited, but she didn't elaborate. What do you want her to say? "I was about to come and you . . ." "Well, good. Your husband seemed kind of mad. Not that he didn't have a right to be."

Again I thought she hesitated. "Paul has a terrible temper sometimes. Don't let it bother you. . . . See you later, then."

45

All day I kept replaying that conversation, rehearing Zoe's soft, slightly questioning voice. She never came right out and sounded on his side nor did she totally take my side, but she was certainly nice about it. Okay, this is absurd, but before going over to walk Baby, I took a shower, splashed myself with Phil's 4711 and even changed my shirt. I know, I know. Still, why look like a teenage slob, even if you *are* just walking a dog?

I let myself into the apartment. It was totally quiet. Was she asleep again? Or had she started feeling so well, she'd gone to class after all?

"Here, Baby," I whispered. "Let's go, okay?"

I closed the door as quietly as possible. It was raining so I'd brought an umbrella, but Baby didn't seem very eager to go across the street to the park side, even though I held the umbrella over him. I decided not to push it. I watched till he'd gone a few times and then headed back. One thing I was sure of: when I got there, I wouldn't do anything as gauche as call out, "It's me! Paul!" I'd just let Baby in, undo his leash and leave, like a man.

But when I returned, Zoe was in the front hall, looking through the mail. She was in a terrycloth bathrobe, just like her husband's. She yawned. "Gosh, I've slept all day, how awful."

I tried to look sympathetic. "You should. It's good for you if you're sick. . . . Do you, uh, need me to go out and get you any orange juice? My father thinks drinking a quart of orange juice a day is the cure."

She smiled. She did look pale, her hair disheveled, but even prettier in a different kind of way, more delicate. I just stood there, staring at her. "I hope you didn't get too wet," she said. Baby was snuggled into his bed again.

"No, I like the rain. It isn't coming down too hard." Suddenly the apartment seemed horribly quiet and I felt like my thoughts were coming out at her through a loudspeaker. *I want you, I love you, I think you're beautiful!*

"So, next weekend will be okay?" she said. "What I thought was, if it's more convenient for you, you could bring Baby to your father's apartment. He likes company. That's why I hate to put him in a kennel because I know they just lock them up in little cages. But my mother-in-law is allergic to dogs. Would that be okay? Would your father mind?''

''He usually stays at his girlfriend's,'' I said, ''but anyway, he wouldn't mind.''

Zoe glanced away. ''Could you take his bed and that blanket? I think that way he'll feel more at home. . . . This is so nice of you! We'll pay extra, of course. Would fifty dollars for the weekend be all right?''

''That sounds like a lot.''

''It's less than we'd pay a kennel. I don't want to exploit you. Anyway, you can probably use the money for dates.''

I swallowed. ''I don't actually go out that much.''

''How come?''

''Well, like I said, I spend a lot of time on my writing.'' Did that sound convincing?

''Are you working on anything special right now?''

''I'm about to hand in a play for school. I have to have it Xeroxed, but, well, basically, it's done.''

''What's it about?''

''Um . . . Well, I guess friendship, but really romance too—that is, can there be both, simultaneously, I mean, or even sequentially. What I mean is, can two people who, can they also—''

Mercifully she cut into this blather and asked, ''Is it autobiographical?''

''In a way . . . Well, yeah, it is. See, I, there was a girl, we used to be friends and then—'' I suddenly stopped short. I didn't know what I wanted Zoe to think of me. Partly I wanted her to think of me as experienced, lots of girlfriends, but I didn't want to overdo it to a point that would seem ludicrous.

''Are you still going together?'' Her voice was soft and caressing. *She's in a bathrobe. She isn't wearing anything underneath, maybe just a nightgown.*

''We never really . . . She liked me more than I liked her. I mean, I liked her, but I wanted to be her friend and she wanted it to be a real romance. I'm afraid I might have hurt her feelings.'' Wait till Sonya reads the play! Still, I felt I

47

was presenting myself well, a heartbreaker, but a sensitive one.

"I had that once with a boy in high school," Zoe said. "He liked me and I . . . I just didn't feel romantic about him. I kept trying to explain. It wasn't that there was anything *wrong* with him, I just didn't. . . . Romance is sort of inexplicable."

"Right." I had the feeling if I stayed with her one second longer in that small dark hall, I would do something insane like fall at her feet or lunge at her like those terrible guys she hated in college. I pulled myself together. "So, I'll go on duty on Friday the eighteenth."

"Great." She smiled. "Wish me luck."

"What about?"

"Visiting my in-laws is the pits. My mother-in-law is always yammering away about my having a child. 'Why aren't you giving us a little heir?' "

"She sounds like a jerk," I said with feeling.

Zoe just smiled. "Bye, Paul."

I love the way she says my name. Paul. Well, she's had a lot of practice. Her father, her brother, her husband. "As soon as you said your name was Paul." I'm glad she didn't name Baby "Paul." Even though "Baby" has to rank among the most repellent of dog names, still, bending down to put on his leash and calling, "Here Paul, good dog," might be more than even I could stomach.

CHAPTER 6

I had my play Xeroxed at a copy center near the bookstore. Tuesday afternoons at the bookstore are slow. The Village crowd tends to come in more at night. It's a small store with a lot of foreign magazines, a big selection of art books, poetry. Sometimes movie stars come in. Madonna came in once, so they said. I was in the basement doing inventory at the time, of course. The story of my life. The other salesclerks are mainly older than me. On Wednesday there's Tina who's a dropout from Oberlin. She's living at home with her parents. I haven't told anyone at the job that I want to be a writer. That sounds like such a cliché. Max, the owner, would probably fire me if he knew. He says most writers should be paid not to write.

Thursday I handed out the copies of *Just Friends* to everyone in Playhouse 74. Luckily, Sonya wasn't there. "I'll give her a copy," Wolf said. "She's not feeling well."

I will have to face Sonya on this sooner or later. Or will I? After all, Sonya is a sophisticated, literary type, right? This is a play. Everything has been changed except for a few conceptual things. Millions of kids are in this situation. One likes the other more, a misunderstanding. It's classic. And it happened almost six months ago. Sonya doesn't give a damn about me anymore. The main thing is, no one but Sonya and I even know it happened! I knew I was getting all wrought up over nothing. I ought to be worrying how the gang will like it. Will they thing it's well-written? *I* think it is, but I'm not exactly objective. Can it be worse than Maria Cantor's play in verse?

Friday night I went to the Bernstein apartment. There was a little note from Zoe with a check for $50. I walked Baby first and then returned for his bed. "See, you're not even leaving the building," I explained. "Our place is just across the lobby. It's practically the same apartment." He stood there, uncertainly, but I scooped him up, put him in the bed, and carried the bed out into the front hall. I set it down and locked the door. Strangely, Baby didn't seem to mind being carried that way. I got a few strange stares from people as I crossed the lobby, but I just smiled insouciantly.

In her note Zoe said she'd fed him for the day. I'd brought the other cans of food in my school bag. I decided I might as well put Baby's bed in my room. That way he'd smell me and feel at home. Smells are important to dogs. He settled right down and went to sleep, even before I fixed dinner for myself. I guess he sleeps a lot. Anyway, I was relieved.

Saturday all went well. I fed him, walked him. I'd re-arranged my bookstore schedule and gone in Thursday. Frankly, Baby didn't seem to know the difference. I talked to him a little, just because Zoe does and I figured he was used to it. He didn't exactly respond, but I'd got the feeling he liked it. Once, as he was eating, he suddenly made this sound as though he was choking. I panicked. Don't let him die, not on this weekend, not when he's with me! She'd never forgive me! I put his bowl of water right in front of him and he took a few laps and quieted down. I looked at him. It's funny. You'd think, feeling the way I do about Zoe, some of that would rub off on Baby. But it hasn't. It's not his fault he's ancient and scraggly-looking and it's not his fault I don't like little dogs. But I feel like I can tolerate his existence and appearance better than when I first saw him. "She loves you more than she loves me," I said to him once and he looked up at me, like: why shouldn't she?

At seven Saturday night, Wolf was coming over with a pizza. I figured he'd have to have read my play. I respect Wolf's opinions, even though he's going to be a doctor. He's more blunt and cut-and-dried than some of the others in the group, but I figure that's good. He's more of a typical educated person who, if I ever get a play put on, will have to want to see it. When we have dinner together, he always gets our special, an anchovy-and-garlic pizza from a place near his house. For most people it's too salty and I admit you're usually up half the night drinking gallons of water. But if you wash it down with a lot of beer while you're eating it and eat it slowly, you're okay.

"Is it still hot?" I asked after I'd let him in. "Should we put it in the oven?"

"Yeah, pop it in for a few minutes." I figured we'd eat in the kitchen at the round wooden table. "I could bring it in my room," I said, "only Baby's in there."

"Who?"

I'd told Wolf about my dog-walking, but maybe I had never explained his name. "She got him when he was a baby."

Wolf crossed his eyes. That's an expression we both use when we're alone, meaning something is beyond belief. Wolf knows nothing about how I feel about Zoe and he won't. It's too stupid to be worth telling him about. Anyway, he doesn't have a girlfriend and never has, in any serious way, so he won't even understand.

As we were eating the pizza, I said, "So, did you get a chance to read my play?" With anyone other than Wolf I wouldn't just blurt it out like that, but I figured with him it was allowable.

He nodded.

"What'd you think?" Already I felt a little anxious. Wolf's usually pretty verbal, even when his mouth is full of pizza.

"As a play?"

I stared at him. "Sure, as a play! I mean, it's not pretending to be anything else."

"As a play, I liked it."

There was something definitely weird going on here. "But as a what you didn't like it?"

Wolf looked away. "It's more Sonya," he said.

Huh? Shit. What does Wolf know about Sonya and me? I never told him—I was a perfect gentleman. "What about Sonya?" I asked. I decided to fake naivete as long as I could.

"She's really angry, Paul. . . . In fact, let's face it, she's furious. She says if we put it on, she's quitting Playhouse 74."

Great, let her quit. "How come? I don't get it."

Wolf looked at me. We have been best friends since we were three. "I know about the whole thing," he said quietly.

"She told you?"

"Yeah, she told me last month, actually. Not because of your play, obviously. She just . . . wanted me to know." Now Wolf was looking strange.

"Why?"

There was a long pause. "She wanted me to know I wasn't the first."

I couldn't believe it. "Are you saying you—"

He nodded.

"You're saying you and Sonya are . . . making it together?"

Wolf gave me his appealing crooked smile. "You could even say we're in love—ta da."

"But you never said anything! Since when? This has been going on under my very nose and neither of you . . . What if I *hadn't* written the play? You *never* would have told me?" It felt great to feel justifiably angry at someone else.

"We haven't exactly kept it a secret. Half the school knows. It's just you've been in such a fog lately."

Me? Fog? "It seems incredible," I muttered. "I can't take it in."

"Are you pissed off?" He looked vulnerable and more like himself. "You had your chance . . ."

"Yeah, but I . . ."

"You said you didn't love her. . . . The guy in the play says it too. 'I'm not in love with you.' Here, page eighteen."

"Why you, though?"

Wolf laughed. "Why *not* me? Am I so hopeless?"

"No, but Sonya . . . Is Sonya what you really want?"

Wolf looked embarrassed. "Yeah, she is."

I raised my beer mug. "Well, good luck and many happy returns of the day!"

"Thanks. . . . But that doesn't get you off the hook about the play."

"What hook? Are you going to hang me? What have I done that's so hideous?"

"Well, for one, you took a very personal, private event which took place between two people and you've turned it into a public event which hundreds of people will see and laugh at and comment on. That's how Sonya feels."

"Why should they laugh?"

"Because it's funny. . . . Look, I like your sense of humor, Paul, but think of it from Sonya's point of view. She feels really betrayed."

I opened a second can of beer. "But, nobody knows except you, me, and Sonya, so what does it matter?"

Wolf looked sheepish. "Well, she also told Gabrielle."

Gabrielle is and has been Sonya's sidekick since they were both in second grade. She's a tall, skinny, brilliant girl with almost albino-white blonde hair. "Anyone else?"

"That's it."

"Okay, so apart from the two perpetrators of the evil deed, we have two confidants, both totally sympathetic to Sonya's point of view. So tell me: where's the humiliation?"

"It's the *way* you've portrayed her. Sonya says that's not what she's really like."

"Like what? What d'you mean?"

"Like her getting all hysterical after you do it, or right after 'Jim' and 'Fiona' do it. She hates the name Fiona, by the way—"

"I'll change it."

Wolf was imperturbably reaching for his third slice of pizza. At least his concern over Sonya's sufferings hadn't taken his appetite away. "It's also—"

"That's your third piece," I reminded him.

"So? Eat! Who's stopping you?"

"I'm losing my appetite." But I reached for another slice. "So, go on—she thinks she *didn't* get hysterical?"

"Did she?"

"No."

"And you give her some brother who supposedly forced her to have incest with him when she was eleven which supposedly has made her frigid and half-insane. She doesn't *have* a brother! She's an only child!"

"It's a play!" I yelled. "It's supposed to be *dramatic*. I had to give motivation. If I just wrote about two teenagers doing it once and then falling asleep, where's the play? Where's the drama?"

Wolf smiled. "You just did it once?"

"Yeah. . . . Scout's honor. Why? Did Sonya say we did it ten times?"

"No, she said once, but I'm trying to get the two versions straight . . . even leaving the play aside."

"Do you want to hear my version?"

He hesitated. "Yeah. . . . I feel like Sonya would kill me if she was here, but—"

"Wolf, what *is* this? We're friends. Is Sonya going to follow you into the men's room from now on? I'm going to tell you the absolute, unvarnished story of what really happened."

"From your point of view, though," Wolf said.

"Whose point of view am I supposed to tell it from? I only *have* one point of view."

"Okay, go on."

Wolf listened while I told it. I really told it just as it had happened, not leaving out anything either in terms of actions or thoughts. When I was done, he said musingly, "It's true, Sonya can't handle liquor. I've seen that. She claims that if she hadn't gotten sloshed, the whole thing might not have happened."

"Possibly. . . . Only she did." I didn't believe that, but if it made Wolf happy to think so, I wasn't going to stop him.

"The other thing," Wolf went on, picking at his crust. "She says you make it seem like she was the aggressor every step of the way. She did this or that, almost like, as Jim says

54

at the end to the audience, it was date rape from the boy's point of view."

"It *was* like that. . . . I'm sorry."

"It takes two to tango. . . . Sonya says you just show that one night. You didn't show the months or years, even, of your flirting with her, making suggestive jokes, telling her your sexual fantasies. *She* says that was all a come-on and that all *she* did was take the final step or make the final suggestion."

I sighed. "Look, Son and I were buddies. I talked to her the way I talk to you."

"You never told *me* about your sexual fantasies." He smiled slyly.

"Okay, maybe there was a kind of flirtatious undercurrent," I admitted. "But she told me hers too! I thought of it as two people of the opposite sex who liked each other enough to be open . . . about everything. I never had that. I'm an only child too, remember. I never had a sister. It was interesting. Sonya's very honest. I never knew girls even thought about it till she told me. She made it seem real, that they masturbate, everything."

Wolf frowned. "What's everything?"

"I just added that on to round off the sentence."

"So she told you *her* sexual fantasies too?" Wolf was looking more and more upset.

"It was just a mutual thing. It was talk. We're talkers. That's probably why we're not suited." Privately I wondered how suited Sonya and Wolf were, but I decided not to offer my opinion on that unless pressed.

"Sonya says you have hang-ups about women. Your whole Jackie Bisset fantasy."

"Why is that a hang-up? Who does she *want* me to have fantasies about? Linda Hunt?"

Wolf laughed. "What she says is, you pretend you're looking for a smart, intellectual, sensitive girl, but then at night you lie there imagining Jackie Bisset in a torn undershirt rolling up on some desert island."

I sighed. "I *am* looking for a smart, intellectual, sensitive girl. If she looks like Jackie Bisset, I won't throw her out of bed. So, sue me."

"What was wrong with Sonya?"

"There's *nothing* wrong with her. I wouldn't have made her happy! She wouldn't have made *me* happy. Something was wrong. Now she has you and she's happy, evidently."

"On the rebound," Wolf said morosely.

"Wolf, what was there to rebound *from*? It was *one time*!"

"She said it wrecked her whole summer."

"It's November now. . . . Who's in the sack with someone else a mere six months later? Her or me?"

Wolf made a wry gesture. "She thinks *you* are."

"*Me?* With who?"

"I don't know. I told her I always assumed you would tell me if—"

"Of course I would," I said, feeling a small spear of guilt shiver through me. "My life right now is school, the bookstore, walking this fucking dog, working on this play which I happen to think is my best play—"

"It *is* your best play," Wolf said.

That made me feel good. We'd gotten so totally sidetracked that I'd almost forgotten that what I really wanted was Wolf's opinion of the play from a literary point of view. "What if I make changes?" I said. "Not major ones, but let's say I let Sonya go through it and red-pencil things she feels violently about. I could change a thing here or there. Like, maybe the brother. It could be her uncle."

"I'll suggest that."

"It means a lot to me to have this put on senior year," I said. "I worked hard on it."

Wolf leaned back in his chair. "Sonya is complicated," he said, but in a completely different voice, almost dreamy. "Sex is complicated. I didn't think it would be."

What I was thinking about was Sonya's assumption that I was making it with someone and Wolf's saying earlier, "You've been in such a fog." Maybe I should tell Wolf about Zoe. But then I realized he'd be bound to tell Sonya who'd tell Gabrielle and . . . "I wish she hadn't picked you," I blurted out.

"Why? Don't I deserve something in my senior year other than working on lung transplants with my father?"

Actually, sex with Sonya might not be unlike doing lung transplants in terms of anxiety level. "I guess I feel like before it was you and me and now your loyalty's shifted. Like with the play. You couldn't just give me *your* opinion. You had to give me *hers*."

"That's a special case," Wolf said.

"I feel like whatever I tell you from now on, say I tell you something personal, you'll go back and tell her."

Wolf held up his hand. "I won't. I swear. Do you have a Bible handy?"

I half-believed him. But what was there to tell? He was having real sex with a real girl and I was having sick, stupid fantasies about a married woman who thought of me as some kid who walked her dog. "At least you're having an interesting senior year," I said. "I'm still living my life at the typewriter."

Wolf smiled. "You'll meet someone, Paul. I know it. Any day now."

I've met her, I thought, but I didn't say anything.

After dinner we watched TV and later in the evening I took Baby down for his final walk. Wolf was already in his pajamas. It was brisk out. I shivered a little. What was Zoe doing now? Was she asleep in her in-laws' guest room? *"She keeps yammering away about my having a child."* A flash-image of Zoe pregnant with a child. No! Her mother-in-law sounds like a perverse beast. She's only twenty-two! When I came back upstairs, Wolf was asleep. Baby scurried into my room and curled up in his basket. He snores in his sleep, not loudly but with little snuffly erratic noises like a radiator starting up.

CHAPTER 7

Wolf left after breakfast, promising to relay the message to Sonya that I was agreeable to making changes in the play if she would do it privately and not make a big stink at the Playhouse 74 meeting the next week. It wasn't until Wolf left, for some reason, that the idea of him and Sonya as a couple began to hit home. Not the fact that my best friend had a sex life and I didn't, not jealousy over Sonya. I guess it was more that first I'd wrecked whatever I had with Sonya, friendship or whatever, and now I didn't even have Wolf in the same way anymore. Sure, he said it was just about the play that he was taking her side, but of course it was more than that. Of course they would talk about me, Sonya analyzing my character in her inimitable way, having all the years of our closeness to draw on for ammunition. I hated the thought of that. Talk about betrayals!

And Wolf, funny-looking little Wolf was the one who . . . But so what? He's right. He got her on the rebound. You didn't want her. You would have made each other miserable. I didn't think I was jealous, but I felt a pang of aloneness. Phil has Jayne, Penny has Mike, Zoe has Paul, *her* Paul . . .

I went to a movie at four, took Baby for his last walk. Zoe had said they'd probably be back in the early evening, and that if they weren't, she'd call me. If I didn't hear from her, I was to assume they would take over from four o'clock on. I brought Baby's bed with me and left it with Pablo while I did the final walk. Then I carried Baby in the bed upstairs again, as I had two days earlier.

When I entered the Bernstein apartment it was dark, of course. Late afternoon, no lights on. I turned on the hall light and set Baby's bed down where it usually was, under the window. Suddenly, for some reason, my heart started thumping wildly. I realized I'd never seen the rest of their apartment. They wouldn't be back for several hours. I walked slowly through the whole apartment. It looked like they'd invested quite a bit in fixing it up. The kitchen was all new and shiny, very unlike Phil's. I'd seen the living room. Pretty standard, but expensive-ish stuff. Leather couches, soft oriental rugs. Not bad. All of this from orthopedic shoes. At least Zoe doesn't wear them.

Naturally I was most curious about their bedroom. It was the same size as Phil's, but they had two beds side by side, each with its own night table. For some reason that pleased me. I realize you can make love just as often with two beds as one, but still someone didn't want the proximity of another body all the time. Who? It had to be Zoe. How could stupid Paul, awful as he was, not want that body next to him? There were two bureaus, a his and hers. It was clear which was Zoe's because it had a big mirror and some perfume bottles on it.

I pulled open the drawers to look at her clothes. *Why am I doing this? Am I crazy? What if they come home?* I looked at everything. Her underwear. A neat pile of silky bikini-style underpants, all in pink, a few bras. 32B. Nothing very fancy or erotic, but to me they were. Then a drawer of nightgowns. Mostly short ones with flowers and matching panties. No slinky black-satin numbers. She doesn't need that. I held them up in front of the mirror. *Does this mean I'm a transvestite?* I imagined Zoe in the nightgowns, imagined I was holding her instead of them. *This is sick. You could get ar-*

59

rested. If they walk in right now, you'd not only be fired from walking Baby, they could call Phil. You could be expelled from school!

But I stayed in the dark bedroom, touching the nightgowns and carefully replacing them one by one. Then I just sat on the edge of the bed and buried my face in my hands. I felt like crying. I just felt so miserable and so pierced with the most mawkish kind of adolescent longing. It isn't fair! What? *I want her to love me. I want her to . . .*

I stood up, shaking my head like a wet dog. *Get out of the apartment. You're just being self-indulgent and ridiculous. Go home and take a cold shower.* Should I leave a note? I found a pencil and wrote:

> Dear Zoe and Paul,
> Everything was fine with Baby. I hope you had a good weekend.
>
> > Sincerely,
> > Paul Gold

Back home Phil had returned, without Jayne. He was in the living room, lying on the couch. "Paul?"

"Yeah, hi."

"Have a good weekend?"

"Pretty good. . . . Wolf came over."

"Come on in here. I can't see you."

I walked reluctantly into the living room. I didn't feel like talking to Phil or to anyone especially.

"Get your play finished?"

I nodded.

"I'd like to read it sometime."

"Okay. . . . I don't know yet if they're going to do it. They're voting next week."

"Of course they'll do it! How can they not do it? You're the best!"

It's true, damn it, I am . . . at least at Hamilton. God, if Sonya makes them not put on my play, I'm going to kill her. I just made a hopeless gesture.

Phil was grinning. "So, guess what? Jayne and I set the date!"

"For what?"

"For getting married! Hey, where are you?"

I tried to pull myself together. "Terrific. When is it?" I tried to sound happy and enthusiastic.

"We thought the day after Christmas. We'll just go to City Hall, and then we'll have a small gathering of people, friends, what have you. Get a nice suit, if you don't have one. . . . So, what do you think? I bet you thought I'd never do it, huh?"

"No, I figured you would, eventually."

"Eventually!" Phil laughed. "Yeah, it was eventually, all right. But, Paulie, let me tell you something. I just wasn't ready till now. All the others—it wouldn't have worked. Not because of them, not because of me. You've got to be ready. Don't do it because some girl pressures you or you feel you should or any damn thing. Listen to the inner voice."

"Sure." I hate it when Phil gives me fatherly advice. He sounds like Polonius come back from the grave.

"Even when the sex is great, be detached. Say: do I really have something in common with this girl, this woman, something deep, something eternal? Do we share the same philosophy of life? Do we—"

"Phil, listen, I don't even have a girlfriend, okay? So all this is like telling a Bowery bum how to arrange his stock portfolio." I liked that analogy, actually. Maybe I could use it somewhere.

"Relax, you will. You're smart. You're ten times smarter than I was at your age. Girls like smart guys."

They do? I thought of the guys in our class who are going with the best girls. They sure aren't the smartest. It sounded like the lyrics to a pop song. *Girls like smart guys*. Sure, they're easier to make asses of.

Phil sat up. "What about, you know the one I mean, the one who was interested in chess, who lives in this building."

"Sonya? She's going with Wolf."

Phil raised his shoulders. "Huh. Unexpected combination. Still, probably everything is, right? Why should a girl like Jayne like me? Look at all the men in New York who're ten million times handsomer than me, richer, more on the ball. . . . But somehow . . ."

There is nothing worse than trying to feel happy for someone like your father or your best friend when deep down you feel rotten. Phil even insisted we open a little bottle of champagne at dinner. I don't even like champagne that much, but I didn't want to be a spoilsport. "Where're you going to live?" I asked.

"Here." Phil looked indignant. "No way am I giving up this apartment. Are you kidding? It's a little far from Jayne's job, but she likes the neighborhood."

"So, where will she put all her stuff?" I had this sudden image of my room, the whole apartment, inundated with crap.

"Well, you'll be away at college next year. We've got a lot of closets. . . ." He looked uncomfortable.

"Well, as long as she doesn't want any kids, I guess it doesn't matter," I said.

Phil actually blushed. "Well, actually . . ."

"What! Don't tell me she's pregnant!" In my senior year: a baby! Oh shit.

"No, don't rush us. But she's in her thirties. Eventually, yes, she wants one. And I wouldn't mind. I'll be a different kind of father. I'll be more involved. You just kind of raised yourself. I admit it. Pen and I were too young. I mean, look at you. You turned out fine. But this time around I'd do it differently, no two ways about it."

"Sounds great," I said sarcastically.

Phil looked annoyed. "You think I'm too old or what?"

"No, I think you're a fine age."

Phil sighed. "It's true. . . . I'll be almost sixty when the kid graduates college. I'll be an old father, like *my* father was, gray-haired, fat, out of it. . . ."

"No. . . . You'll stay thin. You'll be peppy." I felt a perverse satisfaction in watching Phil's ecstatic mood ooze away.

"With a girl it wouldn't matter so much," he said. "Girls are more accepting. But a boy. Boys want you to go out and play baseball with them."

62

"I never did."

"You were different. You were intellectual. . . . Plus, I didn't have the time then, even if you'd wanted. This time around I'll probably have a husky, rough-and-tumble little guy and he'll say, 'Daddy, come on out and hit a few,' and I'll be sitting on the park bench, crippled by arthritis—"

I slapped Phil on the shoulder. I was a little high from the champagne. "You'll be a great father. Don't worry about it."

Phil started clearing the dishes. He looked bemused. "I do hope it's a girl. Girls adore their fathers. You should have seen my sister and my father together. I want that. I want to be adored."

Who doesn't? I thought of Mike saying of Maureen O'Duffy, his high-school sweetheart: *"She made me feel like a king."*

It was ten o'clock. The phone rang. I heard Zoe Bernstein's voice saying, "Hello?"

"Hi, it's Paul."

"I hope this isn't too late. . . . Things were okay with Baby? It worked out all right? I worried all weekend."

"It was fine. He took to it right away."

"I'm so glad. Thanks so much. I really appreciate it."

"Did you have a good weekend?"

She laughed. "Too complicated to go into, but, in a word, yes. . . . I'll see you, then. Take care."

Did I put all her nightgowns back in the right order? Would she notice anything amiss? Would *he*? Papa Bear: *Someone's been sleeping in my bed!* You wish.

CHAPTER 8

Monday afternoon, after classes, there was the Playhouse 74 meeting. Earlier in the day there'd been the voting for which three plays would be put on. The voting is by secret ballot. At the meeting we discuss the plays that won and how we think they should be done. *Just Friends* was one of the three, along with Maria's play in verse and Sherman Lersh's surrealist comedy about the man who discovered bubble gum. I was glad in one way. Mine was the only even semi-realistic play. Of course, it was also the best, but at least Sonya hadn't done any electioneering behind the polls to eliminate me.

I won't bore you with what was said about *Bubbles* or *The Witch of Thornhill Meadow*. I'll get straight to what they said about *Just Friends*. By the way, earlier in the day, Wolf had come up to me and said Sonya agreed to "my terms," that is she wouldn't object if I'd make all the changes she demanded. I hated the idea of Sonya's having that kind of power over my play, but I also counted on Wolf to be some kind of reasonable intermediary.

"I really like this, Paul," Annice said. "It's so funny and

it's so . . . real.'' She blushed. ''I mean, I think that's what relationships are really like.''

Trying not to look at Sonya was like being the man on the bicycle who tries not to look at anything but the tree he's afraid he'll crash into. She seemed to loom at the periphery of my consciousness. ''Thanks,'' I said with fetching humility. ''Is there anything you think ought to be changed?'' I figured if enough people said it was great just the way it was, Sonya's case would be harder to get across.

''Well, I did think the part about her brother, the incest part . . . I mean, you know it's a little heavy. I don't think she should seem crazy. At the end Jim says, 'We're two nice, normal kids,' but how many nice, normal girls have incest for five years with their brother?''

I snuck a very rapid glance at Sonya. She looked pale and her hands were clenched in front of her. ''I agree,'' Wolf said.

I sighed. ''Okay, strike the incest. . . . Any other comments?''

Sherman Lersh has terrible skin and a huge Adam's apple. If he didn't write plays, he'd be one of those strange guys who hooks up his computer to the defense department and inadvertently starts World War Three. ''It just struck me, I hate to be rude, Paul,'' he said in his scratchy voice, lighting up a cigarette, ''but it's so banal. A guy and a girl fuck. And then they're sorry. Or they're not sorry. So what? It's a so-what play.''

I reddened. I didn't know what to say. It's hard to defend yourself when the attack is so general. But Annice rose to my defense. ''It's about real *life*, Sherman! Some people actually *care* about real life. No offense to your play, but Paul is trying to deal with what life is really like for kids like us.''

Sherman snorted. ''But these kids are such jerks! They have no political consciousness. The outside world doesn't exist for them. It's all romance. It's moderately well-written, but it's romance dash sex.''

''Sex is important,'' Wolf said wryly. ''What's wrong with sex?''

Georgia Horowitz, who's generally very quiet, said,

"Anyway, who *says* they don't have any political consciousness? Paul just didn't put that in the play because he wanted to focus on one particular moment in their lives."

"What's worth writing about in this particular moment?" Sherman persisted. The air was getting smoky from his filthy cigarettes. "She gets drunk. She kind of rapes him almost. He's this quintessential wimp, taking no responsibility for his actions. . . . Can't you see all the parents in the audience? This is just what they already think of us and we're telling them it's true!"

Annice was getting quite excited. "I don't think he's a wimp at all!" she cried. "He's sensitive. He's diffident. . . . What do you want him to be—some Rambo-type muscle-bound idiot? This is Hamilton High School! And at the end he says, 'This is just the way *I* look at it,' so he's admitting that there are millions of ways to look at any one situation. That's what Hamlet is like. Is *he* a wimp?"

Wow. Maybe I should have an affair with Annice. But as Zoe said, "Romance is inexplicable." I just don't find Annice sexually attractive. Too bad. "Sherman may be right about Fiona getting drunk," I said. "That might be a little too—"

"Yeah, tone that down," Wolf said.

Then Annice in total innocence looked at Sonya. "What do *you* think, Sonya? Did you like it?" I would swear on my life she asked that just because Sonya usually has a million opinions and this afternoon she hadn't even opened her mouth.

"I think if certain changes are made, it could be . . . okay," Sonya said stiffly.

Sherman was rubbing his hands together in a nervous way he has. "I hate to be crude, but are they actually going to, you'll pardon the expression, 'do it' on stage?"

"No, it's just implied," I said. "The stage will be dark. We'll hear them talking."

"No bedsprings squeaking?" Sherman laughed uproariously. "No heavy breathing?"

If that guy has ever had sex with anyone or anything, I'd consent to withdraw my play immediately. Talk about wimps!

66

To call Sherman Lersh a wimp would be a consummate compliment. Annice sighed. "Sherman, you're really being obnoxious. Paul's play is about a relationship. It isn't even *about* sex."

That was about it. As the meeting ended, Annice said to me, "I really meant what I said, Paul. I thing it's a terrific play."

"Thanks for coming to my defense."

Annice looked around. Sherman had left. "He's such a fool. And *he* writes about bubble gum!"

I wish I could like Annice in a romantic way. I don't. Maybe she was thinking, hoping I would say something more. I just said, "See you."

Outside Wolf and Sonya were standing together. Sonya said to me quietly, "I'll go over the play this weekend."

"Fine."

She looked me straight in the eye. "You're lucky to have a friend like Wolf."

On the way home I pondered that last remark. Meaning if Wolf hadn't pleaded so eloquently in my defense, she would have stopped the play from being put on at all?

That weekend I got Sonya's red-penciled copy of *Just Friends*. It looked like a crazed English teacher had had a hemophilia attack all over it. Red lines, arrows, notes, instructions. Sonya's revenge. I decided to ignore a lot of it and only make the changes that made sense. Playhouse 74 had voted it in. If she didn't like it, she could damn well lump it. As I was returning from walking Baby, I felt a hand touch my arm. It was Zoe Bernstein. "Hi. . . . My teacher was sick today. I went all the way down there for nothing," she said cheerfully.

It was a cold day. She was wearing a sheepskin coat with a hood. Her hair was ruffled from the wind.

"So, how's it going?" she asked.

It's strange how, whenever I'm with Zoe, everything seems very clear and bright; even commonplace things I normally never notice seem surrounded by a halo of significance. "My play was accepted," I said happily.

She gave me a quick little hug. "Oh, terrific! I'm so glad."
We were in front of her elevator. "Come on up and I'll make
you a cup of hot chocolate to celebrate."

"That would be great." This was already the best day of
my life.

I followed her into the kitchen. She flung her sheepskin
coat on a chair. I took my coat off too. Underneath her coat
she was wearing tweed slacks and a white shirt. *Please let
me not say anything stupid. Please let this go all right.* Zoe
set down the cup of hot chocolate in front of me. She'd made
a cup for herself too. Then she sprayed some whipped cream
on top. "I love hot chocolate!" she said.

I just gazed at her. *I love you.* "This is wonderful," I said.
"It's really excellent hot chocolate."

"It's just Nestle's, from a can. . . . Paul, I'd love to read
your play sometime. Would you let me? I'm no great literary
critic, but—"

"Sure, I'd really like you to. It's not great, but—"

"I can tell you're very sensitive. I'm sure it's lovely." That
same feeling I'd had when we'd stood once in the small dark
hall came back, even though the kitchen was brightly lit. I
saw myself holding up her nightgowns in the dark bedroom.
If she knew what I was really like . . .

"How did that weekend go when you went away?" I
asked. "You said it was complicated."

Zoe had a slight white moustache from the whipped cream.
Her tongue nipped out and licked it off. "Well," she said
slowly, looking down. "It's what I said. They think I should
have a baby. And Paul thinks I should. I just don't know.
What do *you* think?"

I was unbelievably flattered that she would ask my opinion. "No, I don't think you should," I said loudly, emotionally. "You're so young. You're still in school."

"They say I can always go back . . . or do both. And Paul
is older. I try to see it from his point of view. He says he
doesn't want to be an old father."

I told her all about Phil and Jayne. She listened with seeming fascination, her big, soft black eyes on mine. "That's
interesting. But for him it's different. And for Jayne too.

She's in her thirties. There's the biological time-clock thing. There isn't for me, not yet. . . . And I don't even know if I'd be good as a mother." She laughed hopelessly.

"Oh, you'd be good," I said. *Lower your fucking voice!* "You'd be great, but . . . you have, like, your whole life ahead of you. You shouldn't tie yourself down so fast."

Zoe made a wry expression. "I think I already did by getting married."

"Well . . ." I looked at her, I knew unless she was as insensate as a rock, she could feel some of the emotion that was pouring out of me. I didn't say anything more, but I kept my eyes fixed on hers.

She looked away and then back at me. "I *was* probably too young," she said very quietly. "I think it may . . . no, I don't mean to say it was a mistake, but I sometimes feel . . ."

I couldn't speak. I just stared at her. *Know what I feel for you.*

Zoe looked like she was going to cry. "I don't know! I feel so mixed-up sometimes, about everything. Not just the baby thing. About everything." A tear ran down her cheek; she didn't even seem to notice.

Impulsively I reached over and took her hand. "That's terrible," I blurted. "I want you to be happy."

"You're so sweet, Paul. You seem so understanding. . . . And you've never even been married."

I laughed. "I'm only eighteen."

Zoe laughed too, and wiped away her tears. "You're just a baby still."

I felt stung, horribly hurt. Before I could even reply, she said quickly, "No, I didn't mean that." She gazed at me intensely, her long dark eyelashes raised again, dreamily. "Are you in love with anyone?"

My mind ran in two directions at once. *If I say, "With you," she'd throw me out.* "No," I said. "I guess . . ."

"It mixes you up," Zoe said. "You make decisions that later seem . . . When I met Paul, he was different, he *seemed* different. *I* was a baby. And I guess he partly liked that, my naivete, my being awed at everything. But I don't want to *be*

69

like that forever! I want to grow, do things! I feel I have so much inside me and I see those mothers sitting in the park with their little carriages and the kids and I think: help!''

"It's your life," I said. I felt strong, manly, protective. "Don't let him railroad you into doing anything you don't really want to do."

"Railroad." Zoe sighed. "That's a good word. That's the *perfect* word. Men can be so . . . Well, I suppose that's what makes them good at running things, like the world or whatever."

"Yeah, but look at the world!" I said with a grin.

She laughed delightedly. "Right. . . . It's a mess, and all because men like Paul who aren't evil or mean, just want their own way, they can't really perceive things from another person's point of view."

"He sounds terrible." I hadn't meant to say anything that extreme, it just came out of me spontaneously.

Zoe looked taken aback. "Oh no, I'm giving you the wrong impression. There's a lot in Paul that's kind and sympathetic. I mean, who was I? Who *am* I? Just a kid from a farm in Pennsylvania. Who am I to be so critical? I can't even decide what to major in! He's already out in the world, doing things. That's what he says: he says I just don't know that much about the real world. I don't! He was the first guy I slept with. . . . That probably seems ridiculous to you."

I tried not to look embarrassed. Every time we got near the subject of sex I felt as though my mind was a transparent globe she could see into perfectly. "Why should it seem ridiculous?"

"I just thought your generation . . . Sex must be more spontaneous, not so much of a big deal. Especially for city kids."

I drew a design with a drop of hot chocolate on the kitchen table. "No, that's just a myth people have. All we do is work hard, get terrific scores on our SATs. Very few kids in my class even date. I'm a perfect example. All I do is write plays, walk your dog, and work in the bookstore."

She looked pleased. "Really? I thought somehow . . .

That isn't how I imagined it. You seem so sophisticated compared to the way I was in high school."

"I do?" *Please, let this go on forever. Let her husband be run over right this second.* The phone rang. I'm terribly sorry, Mrs. Bernstein, but your husband was hit in the head by a carton of orthopedic shoes and . . .

Zoe jumped up to answer the phone. I watched her ass surreptitiously since she was half turned away from me. "Oh hi, Pam. . . . Yeah, we did. Only listen, I have this friend over for coffee so could I call you back later? Right. . . . Yeah, speak to you soon." She hung up and said, "My sister. I'll be back in a sec. I just have to go to the bathroom."

While Zoe was gone, I stood up and stretched. I felt so much nervous tension going through my body that I was sure if I touched something electrical it, or I, would go up in smoke. I glanced at the calendar over the sink. Little scribbled notes in what I assumed was Zoe's handwriting. Then I saw written in on the day after Thanksgiving: "Zoe's 23rd birthday. November 29th." I sat down hurriedly, hearing her footsteps coming down the hall.

But Zoe didn't sit down again. She said, "I guess I should start fixing dinner. But thanks for coming by, Paul. . . . And I meant what I said about reading your play."

"I'll bring it over," I said, jumping up.

We walked to the front hall. Zoe looked up at me. "I'm sorry for . . . pouring all this junk out at you. Sometimes I feel like in the city I don't have anyone to talk to the way I did before. I mean, all my girlfriends live far away and even my sister. So it was good to get someone else's perspective."

"Listen," I said. "Any time. I mean that. Just call me any time you feel like talking. I'm right across the hall."

"Okay," Zoe said softly. "I'll remember that."

Then came an awkward moment. She leaned forward to unlock the door and I reached for the handle so our hands touched and inadvertently, without any forethought, I bent down and kissed her. I ended up kissing her hair on the top of her head. Neither of us said anything and a second later I was standing in the hall. *Oh God, I kissed her.* What's wrong with me? She wanted me to. The way she looked at me.

71

Maybe that's just her expression. She was probably thinking what should she cook for dinner. *She has a husband!* How could I do anything so inept, so . . . "You seem so sophisticated," she'd said.

I felt wonderful. I went down in the elevator with a strange desire to do good deeds, feed the starving, write plays that would uplift the human spirit. On the way across the lobby I ran into Sonya who was coming in from the street. "Oh hi, Paul," she said guardedly.

"Hi Son!" I felt so cheerful it even seemed to me that Sonya was the very person I'd been most hopeful of running into.

"Did you get a chance to look at my comments on your play?"

"Yeah. . . . And they're really terrific. You did an excellent job. It'll be a much better play this way. Much more restrained. You cut out all the unnecessary stuff. I really appreciate it."

As one might expect, Sonya looked at me as though I'd taken leave of my senses. "I was afraid you might—"

"Not at all," I said. "Look, the hallmark of a professional is that they can take criticism. You saw through to the play I really wanted to write, but in my bungling, heavy-handed way, failed to."

I could see Sonya torn between calling my bluff and wondering if I was telling the truth. "There *are* some good things in your play," she said in a quieter voice. "It was just—"

"Yeah, I know," I said. "I'm sorry if . . . But now that you and Wolf—"

"Yes," she said, spearing me with a glance. "That makes a definite difference."

We were at her floor. She exited on that line. I was still mentally back in Zoe's apartment. Maybe, in a weird indirect way, it was because of Sonya I had met Zoe. She was the one who'd noticed the sign in the elevator about Baby and called my attention to it. I'm in such a fog a lot of the time I might never have seen it. Thank you, Sonya.

CHAPTER 9

I felt like Zoe's asking to see my play was the perfect opening to making another move in her direction. What else could I do? Usually she wasn't there when I walked Baby. I knew approximately when she returned from her classes, and I debated pretending to be outside our building at that time. But it was cold and dark in November at five-thirty, and I wasn't sure she always came straight home. Besides, that seemed so artificial.

Also, I had the fact that I knew her birthday. I decided to get her a birthday present and bring it over along with the play. The present was a problem. Anything overdone like perfume or jewelry would be too much. But it shouldn't be a nothing present. It had to say something, but not too much, something she could ignore if she chose, but not if she wanted. A book. I get forty percent off at the bookstore, and a book seemed fitting. Poetry. Something romantic, but special. A hardcover. I spent my break one afternoon looking through all the poetry. Books has a large poetry section, all the small presses as well as paperbacks, Penguins. I leafed through one, then another. Finally I came upon a slim hardcover volume put out by a university press in Massachusetts. *About Love: Love Poems Through the Ages.* I glanced through it. It was only twenty poems, printed on beautiful, thick paper. At the bottom of each page was a small design, like a lithograph. The poems weren't just the usual, "How do I love thee? Let me count the ways." There were quite a few modern poems I hadn't known about, as well as one by e.e. cummings that we'd studied the year before in Modern Lit.

> i like my body when it is with your body.
> it is so quite new a thing.

Was that going too far? She's married, she has a husband. True, she's said some negative things about him, but she also said—what?—he was "kind and sympathetic." That was just because she was afraid she'd gone too far. Look, what are you risking by giving her a book? She's not going to fire you. Nothing ventured, nothing gained.

I glanced at the price. $26.95. Ye gods! For a twenty-five-page book! Yeah, but it's classy, it's distinctive. You want to give her something special. And at forty percent off, it'll be under twenty dollars. Still . . .

I bought it. I wasn't sure if I should write something inside. If I did, her husband might see it. I decided on a card, something simple. In it I wrote,

Dear Zoe,
    Here's my play and a book I thought you might enjoy.
Happy Birthday.

                                                        Paul

I debated "love, Paul," but I decided the contents of the book said enough. Too much probably. I gift-wrapped the book and a copy of the play and then wrapped both in plain brown paper. I took the package along when I walked Baby, the day before Thanksgiving, and left it on her doorstep. What if *he* comes home first? Still, all it said was "Zoe Bernstein" on the outside.

I went home, feeling exultant and pleased. I imagined her face when she opened it (alone). I imagined her smiling, leafing through it, getting that dreamy expression.

Thanksgiving Day I spent at Penny and Mike's. Her parents were there: my grandmother, Rose, who took care of me when I was a baby, and my grandfather, Will, who has Parkinson's disease and drools when he eats and never says anything. Mike's parents are younger and louder and he also has two married brothers so the whole event was pretty hectic. Grandma Rose is the only one I really know at all. She's still pretty lively for seventy-two, travels a lot, tutors Chinese scientists who come over here for a couple of years but don't know English that well. She and Grandpa Will were Communists in the thirties and they're still waiting for the revolution.

"So, what's new with school?" she asked me. She's a little hard of hearing. You have to pull your chair close to her. It was after dinner and everyone had dispersed, the men to watch a football game, the younger women, including Penny, to clean up in the kitchen.

"I wrote a play," I said. "They're doing it at Hamilton in the spring."

"So, where's my ticket?"

"You'll get one, don't worry."

Grandma Rose used to let me dictate my stories to her when I was little. She thinks I'm a genius. How can I not like her? "What's it about?"

"A boy, a girl, love, all that . . ."

She laughed. "All that! What do you know about all that?"

I felt annoyed. "What do you mean, Grandma? I'm eighteen. You were *married* at eighteen!"

"But your generation . . . You're too smart for that. Maybe you're too smart for your own good."

"Maybe," I concurred.

"What's new at home? Anything special?" Years ago Grandma Rose hated Phil for supposedly wrecking Penny's life, but now I guess she's mellowed about it. "What's with your father?"

"He's getting married."

Grandma Rose let out a hoot. "Married!" She yelled into the kitchen. "Penny, did you hear that? Phil's getting married!"

Penny came rushing out, a dish-towel in one hand. She was wearing a blue dress that was a little too tight, but she looked pretty and sweaty, dots of perspiration on her shiny pink face. "You didn't even tell us. To who?"

I was embarrassed. Somehow I'd assumed Phil had told them. "To Jayne, this woman he's been seeing."

Penny closed in on me. "Is she nice? What's she like?"

"Is she Catholic?" Grandma Rose asked.

"Mom, he made that mistake once," Penny said. "I bet he picked a Jewish girl this time, right?"

"Why should he pick a Jewish girl?" Grandma Rose retorted. "The mistake was you were too young."

"Yeah, Jayne's Jewish," I said. "She's a physiotherapist. She works with people who have muscular problems as a result of illness or accidents. . . . And she's tall and has brown hair."

Penny was frowning "Is she right for Phil? Are they a good combination?"

"Sure, I guess. . . . I mean, he waited a long time. She's smarter than he is." Why am I saying that about my own father?

Grandma Rose was shaking her head, looking grave. "Uh oh. Trouble . . . The wife should never be smarter than the husband."

"You've always been smarter than Grandpa," Penny said saucily.

Grandma Rose grinned. "True."

"In lots of ways I'm smarter than Mike," Penny said. "Seriously. Not in all ways. But in some ways . . . So, when's the wedding?"

"Around Hanukkah," I said.

"He means Christmas," Penny explained to Grandma Rose.

"I know what he means! . . . So, she's a nice girl and all is well. Are they going to have kids?"

Penny nudged Grandma Rose. "Mom! How should Paul know? Don't keep asking him embarrassing questions."

"At my age you can ask whatever you want," Grandma Rose said.

"I think, yeah, Phil said eventually they want kids." I told her. "She's in her thirties."

"You've got to give him credit for that, Mom," Penny said. "He could've picked some kid in her twenties."

"Phil's got sense," Grandma Rose said, a touch grimly.

Penny went into the living room. "Hey Mike, Phil's getting married."

Mike was intent on the football game. "So?"

"So? Is that all you can say?"

"Hon, it's great, okay? Will you move? You're blocking the set."

Penny came back, fuming. " 'You're blocking the set.' Men! Paul, tell Phil we're really happy for him. Tell Jayne too. Why shouldn't he be happy? *I'm* happy."

"I'll tell him," I promised.

It's funny. All the time now, no matter where I am or what I'm doing, I'm thinking about Zoe. It's like she's there, partly watching the scene with me, partly just there, in some amorphous way. At night, of course, it's worse, because that's all I can think about. But during the day it isn't even a bad thing. I can still concentrate in class, but it makes everything different. She's never met Phil or Penny or Wolf or Sonya. Really, she doesn't know much about me. But, for that matter, I guess I don't know that much about her. Except I feel like I do. I feel like in some ways I know everything, like I could write a play about her and Paul, *her* Paul, how they met, how he snowed her with some idiot male garbage, how she was uncertain inside, but felt it was an opportunity she couldn't pass up.

Two days passed after I dropped off the package and there was still no word from her. I began worrying. Maybe he'd come home first, opened it and thrown it out. Maybe he hadn't even let her know it had arrived. No, it's a holiday. She just hasn't had time to read the play. I gave her the original version of the play because, despite what I said to Sonya,

I think it's better than the revised one I handed in. Will this spoil Zoe's image of me as a sophisticated, sensitive male? Maybe she'll think it's a dumb play. . . . How about the poems? How could I do something that extreme? I should have just sent her a box of chocolates or some flowers. *I like my body when it is with your body* . . . Shit.

The Saturday after Thanksgiving Phil and Jayne gave a party to celebrate their engagement. They invited about fifty people so it got fairly noisy after an hour or so. I know most of Phil's friends, but I didn't feel like staying around for the whole evening. I had some snacks and a few beers. One thing about Phil: he stays friends with his former girlfriends. There were about four of them at the party. One of them was the ex-stewardess, Cindy, who, judged purely by looks, has to be the best of the lot. She has blond hair, hanging loose to her waist, and a perfect body, a lot softer and rounder than Jayne's. She was Phil's girlfriend when I was around thirteen. Just looking at her used to make me have an erection. I used to run when I saw her coming. One night she stayed over and I ran into her on the way to the bathroom. It was the middle of the night. She was coming out of the bathroom and I was going in. She was in a semi-transparent lavender gown. That moment provided material for five years of wet dreams.

"So, how've you been, Paul?" she asked. We were in the kitchen. She was drinking white wine. I think she may have been a little high from the way her words slid together.

"I've been fine," I said.

"Still writing?"

"Yeah. . . . How about you?" Cindy used to write poetry. She showed me some of it. It wasn't as bad as you might expect.

"I got a poem published. . . . Just in my hometown paper, but still. You've got to start somewhere. Right?"

"Right." Somehow she still made me nervous. She was wearing a low-cut white dress. "Are you, uh, married or anything?"

She laughed. "No, I don't seem to have any luck with men."

"Really?" I swallowed, trying not to look below her neck. "That's hard to believe."

"The guys who go after me see me just as tits and ass," Cindy said, her mouth slightly parted. "They don't care if I write poetry. They don't care anything about the *real* me." Her voice was loud, either because she was drunk or because there was so much noise from the party.

"They sound like jerks," I said intensely.

She leaned over and kissed me. "I want someone like you," she said, "only my age. I'm twenty-eight. People say I look younger. Do you think I do?"

Someone like me! "Definitely. . . . *Much* younger."

"My girlfriend likes a guy who's four years younger than she is and they seem so happy. What difference does it make? Women live longer anyway."

"Right," I said. I felt dizzy, either from Cindy's leaning up so close to me or the topic we were discussing or maybe one too many beers.

"Tell me about your love life," Cindy said in her purring, slurred voice. "Are you in love?"

"Yeah, I am," I was amazed to hear myself say. "I'm madly in love with someone."

Cindy smiled. "It's the pits, isn't it? . . . Half the time you feel like you're on speed, the other half—" She made a gesture to indicate a plane dive-bombing.

By now I know I was slightly high myself. There was something about the peculiar intimacy of having a conversation like this with someone I hardly knew, whom I'd probably never see again, in a room full of people, that was a kind of peculiar turn-on. "I gave her this present for her birthday," I said, "and now I'm afraid I overdid it. It was a book of love poetry. Do you think that was going too far?"

Cindy's eyes were gleaming. "Oh no, that's a wonderful present. . . . Why should it be going too far?"

"She doesn't know I love her."

"Now she will." Cindy sipped from her almost empty wineglass. "I love it when men make romantic gestures like that. See, that's what I meant before. Most of them don't anymore. They don't realize women need that. We need romance. We need someone to make us feel we're special.''

"This is one of the poems in the book," I said. I recited the e.e. cummings poem.

> "i like my body when it is with your
> body. it is so quite new a thing.
> muscles better and nerves more.
> i like your body. i like what it does,
> i like its hows, i like to feel the spine
> of your body and its bones, and the trembling
> -firm-smooth ness and which i will
> again and again and again
> kiss, i like kissing this and that of you,
> i like, slowly stroking the, shocking fuzz
> of your electric fur, and what-is-it comes
> over parting flesh . . . and eyes big love-crumbs,
> and possibly i like the thrill
> of under me you so quite new"

I must admit I was not only a bit crocked by now, but rampant strains of horniness kept wafting in and around my body. When I finished, I was afraid Cindy would slug me, but she said softly, "Gosh, that's beautiful. . . . I wish *I* could write a poem like that. . . . He's the one who never uses capital letters, isn't he?"

Just then Phil came by. He looked a little high himself. He slapped me on the back. "So, Cin, how do you like the way he's turned out? Remember what a shrimpy little kid he used to be?"

"He was just shorter," Cindy said diplomatically. "I always knew he'd be terrific once he grew up. Now he's a real man."

Phil winked at me. "And what he needs is a real woman."

"Dad!"

"Okay. . . . He thinks I embarrass him by saying and doing stupid things." Phil grinned. "Are you having fun, Cin? Isn't this a great party?"

"I'm really happy for you, Phil," Cindy said in what seemed to me a sad little voice.

80

"Your time will come," Phil said.

Cindy was pouring herself some more wine. Her red-blond hair drifted down over her eyes and she brushed it back. "I wonder."

"Guys are scared of you," Phil said. "See that guy over there?"

"Which one?" Cindy squinted. Then she quickly took her glasses out of her purse, put them on, and repeated, "Which one?"

"The tall one in the red shirt. He thinks you're dynamite. Selby Rathe. He's dying to meet you, but he's scared."

Cindy slipped her glasses back in her purse. "He looks cute."

Phil grabbed her by the hand. "So, come on over. He may faint when he sees you coming, but we'll bring him to."

They walked off, leaving me standing there. Thanks a lot, Dad. But, after all, this party was for Phil and Jayne and their friends. I was just a teenage kid who'd wandered in. I knew I should go to sleep except I doubted I could with all the noise. I felt lonely and bereft.

The phone rang, but no one else heard it with all the noise. I picked it up. "Hello?"

"Hello. . . . Is Paul Gold there?"

Zoe! "Yeah, um, this is me. Zoe?"

"Oh Paul, hi. . . . I can hardly hear you. We seem to have a bad connection."

"No, it's just . . . My dad is giving a party. Just a sec." I took the phone which has a long extension cord and went into the front hall closet. I closed the door. It was stuffy and dark, but quiet. "Hi," I said, sitting on the floor, shoving the boots to one side. "Is that better?"

"Much. . . . Well, I just wanted to thank you for the lovely gift. Gifts, I mean. I was so surprised! How did you know it was my birthday?"

"I saw it written on your calendar that time we had hot chocolate."

"Well, it was very thoughtful. I haven't had time to read your play yet, but when I do, maybe you can come over and we can talk about it. I looked through it. It looks very interesting."

It was stifling in the closet. I thought I might pass out, and yet there was something exciting about having this secret conversation out of sight of everyone. "It's just a first draft," I said softly. Someone's fur coat was brushing against my cheek. It felt like human hair, silky. "I'm going to rewrite it."

"Next week I have exams," Zoe said. "But maybe after that . . ."

How about the love poems? Didn't you get those?

"What I was calling about, was, well, Paul and I are going to a shoe convention next Friday and I wondered if you could take over. We'll be back Saturday afternoon, so it'd just be for Friday evening and Saturday during the day. Would that be okay?"

"Sure, fine. Where's the convention?"

"Miami Beach. . . . I've heard it's pretty tacky."

"Well, have a good trip."

"Thanks. . . . And thanks again for the presents. Bye."

I put the phone back on the hook and then I sat morosely in the closet. I wanted to die. She didn't even *care* about the love poems! She didn't say one damn *word* about them! She was so cool, so distant. . . . Look, is it her fault you've worked this up into a huge scenario? To her you're a sensitive, sweet kid who walks her dog. Period. End of sentence, end of paragraph, end of topic. I jumped. The phone was ringing again, in my lap. Maybe it was Zoe again. "My husband just stepped out so I wanted to call you back and tell you that . . ."

It was a strange guy, saying in a deep voice, "Is Patti there?"

"I don't know," I said, "I'll look."

I crawled out of the closet, set the phone back on the kitchen counter and went over to Phil. "There's a guy on the phone wanting someone named Patti."

Phil made his hands into a megaphone. "Hey Patti! It's your husband or boyfriend or someone!"

Without waiting to see who Patti was, I went into my

room. Before turning on the light I saw a couple in a tight embrace somewhere near the window. Christ. I coughed loudly. "Uh . . . sorry folks, this is my room. I have to go to sleep."

They broke hastily apart. As they moved toward the door, I recognized Phil's college roommate, Madison, who's divorced, and one of Phil's other ex-girlfriends, Coral. Take her to your own lousy apartment, I wanted to say. Stop polluting my bedroom! You're just jealous. Damn right I am. I flung myself onto the bed. I thought of Cindy and her great body and tiny naive mind and of Zoe, with her gentle, questioning voice. Look, she *couldn't* mention the love poems. Her husband was probably right in the next room. So, why didn't she call me when he wasn't there? Maybe the present embarrassed her. Maybe she's trying to discreetly tell you to bug off. "I have exams next week . . ." What a stupid excuse! Just say: Bug off.

The phone rang again. Without thinking I picked it up, expecting it to be one of Phil's friends again. "Paul?" It was Wolf.

"Yeah, hi. . . . How's it going?"

"You sound funny."

"No, it's just Phil's having a party. I'm a wee bit sloshed, but otherwise—"

"I just had this really stupid fight with Sonya," Wolf said glumly. "I feel rotten."

"What about?" At least someone else was miserable. I was delighted.

"I don't know. It wasn't even . . . she can be so . . . I just said some little thing and she went off like a firecracker, said I was sexist and impossible. I mean, it was ten minutes after we'd just . . . And I was just lying there, feeling great. Maybe I said she had a beautiful body. I don't even *know*! But she got so furious I thought she was going to kill me."

"What'd you say back?"

"I didn't get a chance. . . . I kept trying to calm her down and finally she flounced out of the apartment."

"Where are your parents?"

"At a party."

I was silent. Ten minutes ago they'd been making love. A beautiful body. "She'll get over it. Son's like that."

"I know this is going to sound stupid, but I feel jealous when I think of how close you guys were. Like all that sexual fantasy stuff. She says she's never had that kind of closeness with anyone."

"Really?"

He sighed portentously. "Let's face it, she went after me on the rebound. If you wanted her back—"

"Wolf, it's not a *matter* of back! I never *had* her! You and Son have a real thing. I don't have anything and I never did— with her or anyone else."

I guess the bitterness in my voice got through to him. "Isn't there anyone you—"

"Yeah," I said savagely. "There's someone who thinks I'm a total and absolute jerk, who wouldn't even deign to—"

"From school?"

"No."

"Does she know you like her?"

"If she doesn't, she's the biggest idiot that ever lived. I got her a thirty-dollar book of love poems for her birthday and she didn't even thank me for it." Not true. She did.

"Who *is* she?" Wolf asked, clearly curious.

"I can't tell you. It doesn't matter. She's one of several million women on this planet who don't know I'm alive. She's in excellent company. And forget all that bull from Sonya about how close we were. She's just doing it to make you jealous. She's a jerk too."

"No, she's not. . . . Paul, I'm in *love* with Sonya. She's not a jerk. She just has a hot temper."

I stared at the ceiling. "She'll make it up with you. She's probably trying to phone you right now only the line's busy."

"You think so? Okay, I'll get off, then. . . . But listen, don't worry about that other girl. There are many fish in the sea." That used to be one of our favorite quotes.

"I know, only most of them are fish." That was the rejoinder.

Still, I hung up feeling infinitesimally better. When I'm a

famous playwright, I'll write about this, and people will think what a fool Zoe was, what an opportunity she missed. *His body was found in the East River. One of his neighbors, Mrs. Zoe Bernstein, whose dog he walked, was quoted as saying, "I had no idea how depressed he was. Paul always seemed to be an unusually sensitive, brilliant, amazing young man. What a tragedy for all of us, for the world . . ."*

CHAPTER 10

As the poets say: life went on. The following week, Phil, passing my bedroom and seeing me writing something, said, "Is that your essay for Yale?"

"Huh?"

He repeated it.

"No, I haven't done it yet."

Phil looked horrified. "Paul, it's almost Christmas! Have you done the others?"

Just for the record—I'm applying to Swarthmore, Yale, Sarah Lawrence and, for some reason, Reed, which is out in Oregon. I shook my head.

Phil charged into the room. "What's wrong with you? They won't *take* you if you don't write those essays! The essays count a lot. What's the problem? Can't you think of what to say?"

"I just haven't gotten around to it. . . . I will."

Phil's face was turning purple. "Listen, kid, you get those essays done by the end of next week or that's it. . . . You're moving out."

I laughed nervously. "Where am I moving to?"

"To Penny and Mike's. Wherever. . . . What are you trying to do? Wreck your life? You've had a great education, you did well on your SATs, what *is* this? Some kind of craziness? I'll help you. Tell me what you're going to write about."

God, I was afraid he might have a stroke on the spot. "Phil, I'll *do* them, okay?"

"Do you swear? I'm not joking around, Paulie."

I raised my hand. "I swear on all that's holy . . . on October days, E. B. White, Cindy Moscowitz's tits . . ."

Phil grinned. "You get going. Forget Cindy's tits. You're too young for all that."

I rolled my eyes. "Gimme a break, Daddy." I only call him Daddy when I want to rile him.

But after Phil had departed, I realized he was right. I wondered if it *was* self-destructiveness. I just figure I'll get in somewhere good, maybe even without working too hard on the essays, but I know it's true, the essays are important. "Tell about an event which you feel significantly changed your sense of values." All the topics, either the ones they gave me or the ones I've thought up, seemed banal and absurd. But I have an ability which has served me in good stead all through school. If I decide to, I can sit down and block out everything and write a serviceable essay on any topic. Maybe not the world's greatest, but I just shut off the sarcastic, probing part of my mind and turn into a little turd of a scholar, quoting from obscure philosophers. Just enough bullshit to seem unworldly, but with enough practical hardheaded junk so they know they aren't getting a certifiable screwball.

By the end of the week I'd done all the essays. I left Xeroxes on Phil's desk. He came in later and said, "See? I knew you could do it. These are great. I couldn't have done these. Why do you drive me crazy, Paulie? Why are you still doing that?"

I shrugged.

"Does it bother you that I'm getting married? Jayne thinks it must. All these years, just the two of us, batching it and now—"

"It doesn't bother me, really. . . . I won't even be here. I'll be at college."

"That's what I told her. But she says deep down—first Penny deserted you by marrying Mike, now me . . ."

"I'm fine, seriously. I'm just lazy at times. I've been worrying about my play."

I hate to pull that on Phil, but I truly didn't want to go into the thing with Zoe. "Yeah, that's right. I haven't read it yet. Is it good?"

"It's great." I grinned. "It's frighteningly good."

"Cindy was really impressed by you, how mature you seemed."

"How'd she do with the guy in the red shirt?"

"Shelby? I don't know, frankly. I haven't spoken to him. . . . Cindy's a little mixed-up."

"You gave up a whole stewardess?" That's one of Phil and my favorite lines from *Cactus Flower*.

"Jayne has everything," Phil said, his eyes moist. "I'm a very lucky guy."

I went down to mail off the college applications and stopped by to give Baby his four o'clock walk. Since the Bernsteins would be back the next day I decided to leave him at Zoe's house and just return at eleven to give him the final brief walk before he or I went to sleep.

I ate alone—Phil and Jayne were out—and read a little, fell asleep in front of *Casablanca*, and woke up at ten-forty in a daze. I jumped up and raced across the lobby. I let myself into the Bernstein apartment. One light was on. I walked hesitantly into the living room. Zoe was lying curled up on the couch, watching *Casablanca*. She was in a nightgown, a wool afghan drawn up to her waist. She started when she saw me. "Oh God, Paul . . . Oh, thank heaven it's you. I got so scared. With Paul away, I'm always so nervous."

"What happened to the convention?"

"I just didn't feel up to it. I have a midterm in Psych next week, a twenty-page paper on Arthur Miller for Drama, I woke up with a headache this morning and I thought: I just can't take the time!" Her voice rose desperately. "This is my second chance. I flubbed the first one, maybe because of meeting Paul, all that. I just *have* to prove to myself that I can do it.'' She was almost crying.

"Of course you can do it," I said. I sat down in a comfortable leather chair about six feet from the couch. I glanced nervously at the TV. Zoe had flipped off the sound, but I know the soundtrack by heart. Claude Rains was just saying to Humphrey Bogart, "How extravagant you are—throwing away women like that. Some day they may be scarce."

"I don't know." She seemed in such despair over the fear of possibly not doing well at college that the situation of me walking in and finding her in a nightgown with her husband away didn't seem to bother her at all. She didn't seem embarrassed or awkward. *She thinks of you as a kid brother. You could walk in with her naked and she wouldn't care.* "I don't think you can understand this, Paul. You've probably always done well at school. It comes easily to you. You sit down, you do it. My sister was like that. I'm not. It's a struggle. I try and try, but somehow the words don't seem to fit together. Like this essay on Arthur Miller. His plays aren't obscure, but I can't seem to—''

"Which ones are you concentrating on?" I was trying to ignore the situation as much as she was, which was impossible, but I wanted to at least give that impression.

"Well, *Death of a Salesman*, and—''

"It's a crummy play," I said vehemently. "Forget Arthur Miller! He's a fool."

Zoe's eyes widened. "Really? But it's a classic. My teacher said—''

"It's banal. It's about some schmucky little nothing of a guy whose wife is less than nothing. Miller is like Inge and all those guys in the forties! Now I'll provide motivation! The brother saw his father screwing some broad when he was a teenager and as a result he's warped for life. It's, like, for two-year-olds!" I was warming to my subject . . . pleased she'd picked something I cared about.

"Well, who *do* you like? Or don't you like anyone?"

89

"I like Stoppard, Caryl Churchill, David Hare. . . . I like people who take risks." Except in life.

There was a long pause. My heart was thumping a mile a minute. Thank God I'm only eighteen. Otherwise I'd definitely have a heart attack. Zoe was staring at me pensively. "I read your play," she said. "*Just Friends*. I—I really liked it. . . . You said it was autobiographical, didn't you?"

"Kind of." I told her an abridged version of "my night with Sonya." "Now she's going with my best friend so she doesn't care that much."

"She didn't care that you wrote the play about her?" Zoe looked surprised.

I turned red. "Well, she cared, yeah. . . . She wanted some changes, but I made them and now everything's fine."

Zoe sighed. It wasn't even a sigh, just an exhaling of breath. "In some ways I thought the hero—Jim—was a little cruel to her. Maybe men are just like that if they don't like the woman as much as she likes them. But he just says, 'I'm not in love with you.' That seemed sort of harsh, given it was the morning after and all."

"Should he have lied?" I felt hot, defensive. "I thought that would have been crueler. Isn't it more honest to say what you really feel?"

Zoe looked at me and then away. "I don't know," she said softly.

Another pause descended on us, this time a more paralyzing one that threatened to sever my vocal cords completely. I felt like my breath was going peculiarly. "Did you—uh—like the book of poems?" I asked, feeling like I was leaping in slow motion into a vat of boiling oil.

"Yes. . . . They were lovely." Zoe's hand moved to her throat, then down to the afghan. Her voice was barely above a whisper. "I just . . . I wasn't sure how you meant them."

I swallowed. "I wanted . . . to give you a nice present."

We were staring at each other, like we would each disappear if our glances broke. "It was." Her voice was shaky. "It *was* a nice present."

I knew that the next pause would be like the ice age. It

could envelop the room and us and leave us both stranded here forever. "I wanted you to know how I feel about you." *Jesus, did I really say that?*

Somehow her nervousness was like a balance board which kept me afloat. "Have I been . . . Do you think I've been leading you on?"

"Not if it's the way you really feel."

Zoe looked away and then back, a frightened expression in her eyes. "I'm married!" she said hopelessly.

I half-smiled. "I know." Suddenly I got up and walked over to the couch. I kneeled next to it and without giving myself one second for doubts, I leaned over and kissed her, very tenderly, on the lips. There was a second when her mouth remained closed and then it opened and her arms went around my neck. *Is this happening? Is it a hallucination?*

We paused for breath. I sat back on my heels, just a few inches from her. "This is terrible," she said, laughing nervously. "This is the worst thing I've ever done. *I'm* married, *you're* just in high school. There are probably a million laws against this."

I leaned forward and kissed her again, this time holding on to her bare shoulders. When we came out of that one, Zoe had that dreamy expression.

"Paul, I don't know. . . . I really don't. What do *you* want to do?"

I laughed. "You have three guesses."

"But my husband—"

"Is at this moment giving an eloquent speech on the manufacture of and importance of orthopedic shoes, fifteen hundred miles from here."

Zoe was laughing nervously again. It reminded me of second grade when Wolf used to tell absurd jokes in assembly, daring me not to crack up. A couple of times we were expelled from the room for disorderly conduct. "But he still exists," she said wryly.

I reached for her. "No, he doesn't. He's a figment of your imagination." For some reason, as I stretched out next to her on the couch I remembered that I hadn't walked Baby yet.

"Maybe *you're* a figment of my imagination," Zoe said softly. We were half-entwined. She had given up the struggle.

"No, I'm real. . . . Feel me. Anywhere. I won't disappear."

But we both did. We disappeared and the room and the world and everything in it: husbands, dogs, college, my parents. And when I came to I knew it wasn't the same world and never would be again. Zoe was resting her head on my chest. Her body was just the way I'd imagined it, but better because it was real. She had a freckle under her left breast. For some reason we both looked up at *Casablanca* which was still going, without the sound. "I think this is the beginning of a beautiful friendship," I said, as Claude Rains and Humphrey Bogart walked off together.

Zoe reached over and pressed a button which eradicated the visual as well as the sound effects. "But how *can* it be?" she said, her mouth against my neck.

"It has to . . . we've got to. This will never happen again to either of us." I was speaking with incredible clarity, but that was how I felt. I could have given the keynote address at the Democratic convention without notes, right that second.

"It *has* happened to me before," Zoe said. "With Paul, it—"

"He's a jerk," I said angrily. "He's just some guy you married. You were too young. You didn't know what you were doing."

Zoe sat up. "Paul, no. You're exaggerating. Some of that is true, but he's *not* a fool. He can be stubborn and narrow at times. It's true he voted for Reagan, but—"

"You married a man who voted for Reagan?" I was horrified.

Zoe looked abashed. "He thought his economic policies were—"

"How does he make love to you? Often? Is it any good?"

"It's okay, it's . . . pretty frequent. We're married. It's different when you're married."

"How often?" I persisted.

"Once a week, maybe twice."

God, what an unbelievable schmuck this man is! "And is it wonderful? Do you love it?"

Zoe stroked my hair. "Paul, you're comparing it to . . . When you're in high school, the guy wants to score and he thinks: wow, if I could only do this ten times a day. But when you're married it's different. He's tired and he's thinking about profits and losses and inventory and I'm thinking about whether I'll pass my Psych exam. . . . People who go through life wanting that kind of high all the time are crazy."

"Then I'm crazy," I said. I felt great. This must be what heroin is like. I felt invincible. "I want that. I don't want to settle for anything else."

Zoe smiled tenderly. "No, you're not crazy. You're just young."

"Young! So what are you? Middle-aged? You're, what—four and a half years older than me? You said you never did it with anyone but him before. It's not like you're some experienced woman in a veiled hat with a cigarette holder. There's no difference between us."

"Yes, there is! . . . There's a difference between people who are married and people who aren't. I'm not saying we're better. Maybe we're worse. Like me—maybe I opted for security instead of finding myself."

I ran my hand down her body. "I found you. . . . That's the luckiest thing that ever happened to me."

We kissed. This time Zoe was the one who opened my mouth and ran her tongue greedily along my teeth, and the top of my tongue. She was the one who reached eagerly down my back to my buttocks. The second time we made love was different. I knew it was happening. I let myself detach just a little, just so I'd remember, in case we never did it again. I wanted every moment implanted like a cassette in my brain. Afterward I stood up and started putting on my clothes.

Zoe looked startled. "Where're you going?"

"I have to walk Baby."

"Oh God, that's right. It's pouring, though. Take the umbrella in the hall."

"I brought one."

Baby was no more enthusiastic about going out on a cold, rainy December night than I was. It seemed like I stood on the street forever, mainly trying to hold the umbrella over him. It was half broken, as most of Phil's and my umbrellas are. I returned, my hair soaking wet, shivering.

Zoe was still in the living room, but she'd gotten dressed. Just in jeans and a T-shirt, but still I was taken aback. "Are you going somewhere?" I said ironically. I sat down next to her.

She looked like she was gearing herself up for a speech. "Paul, look, while you were down with Baby, I was thinking. This is all my fault. I *did* lead you on. I do—you are—I *do* find you terribly attractive. Okay." She raised her hand. "I confess. . . . But this is wrong. We can't do it again. I couldn't live with myself. I'm not this kind of *person*."

I felt I understood why people in love kill each other. "*What* kind of person?" I said bitterly. "Someone who's capable of love and passion, who doesn't want to be fucked perfunctorily by some half-comatose businessman once a week?"

"You're talking about sex," Zoe said sharply. "But there's more to life than that."

"I'm talking about life! I'm talking about *your* life! You need me. You're dying in this stupid, expensive, over-decorated apartment."

"Well—" Her eyes started getting that melting, uncertain expression.

I jumped up and started taking off my clothes. Zoe looked scared. "What are you doing? Paul, stop!"

"I'm spending the night."

"But what if—"

"When is he due back?"

"Tomorrow at four."

"I'll leave at eleven." I was naked. It was the first time in my life that I felt glad I was thin and in decent shape. Not muscular maybe, but at least not paunchy and flabby.

"How about your parents?"

"Phil's at Jayne's. . . . Penny and Mike are probably sound asleep or watching some idiot thing on TV."

Zoe giggled. "You're practically an orphan." She went in and got a towel and started rubbing my hair dry. "Poor little wet orphan."

CHAPTER 11

December 9th was the beginning of my life. Everything that happened before that didn't count. I decided that, with my first million, I would give money to New York City to erect a giant statue of an orthopedic shoe in the middle of Central Park. If she'd married the guy I'd imagined Paul Bernstein to be, none of this would have happened. If she hadn't had a dog . . . If they hadn't happened to get an apartment in this building . . . I don't believe in predestination. I believe all of this happened for the craziest, most unlikely of reasons. But it happened. Who cares why?

Paul Bernstein leaves for work every morning at six forty-five. As luck (mine) would have it, he has to be at the warehouse every day. He's a very punctual person. Zoe says he's never missed a day of work since she met him. He never gets sick. At seven-fifteen I cross the lobby, dressed for school, carrying my schoolbooks, and go to their apartment. I let myself in. Zoe is still in pajamas or a nightgown, reading *The New York Times*, having coffee and a donut. We go into their bedroom and make love. She says that when they do it, they always do it in his bed. When we do it, we do it in her bed. I like that better. She says at night she lies there and it's like she can still feel the imprint of my body.

Then, precisely at eight-fifteen, I get dressed and head off for school. Usually I hate winter, I hate the cold, but this winter every day seems excitingly, piercingly cold, the sky bright blue. When the air hits me, leaving her apartment, I feel like it's champagne running through my body. I cheerfully wave goodbye to Pablo, I bounce along the street. Sometimes I walk through the park, but usually I spend all the time I can with Zoe and end up racing for the bus.

One morning, just before Christmas vacation, I ran into Sonya on my way out of the building. She looked at me curiously. "Why are you coming from that side of the building?" she asked.

"The dog," I stammered. "I walk that dog. Remember the sign we saw?"

"Oh, right. . . . What kind of dog did it turn out to be?"

"It's a great dog," I said fervently. "Small, and old, but extremely intelligent."

Sonya looked at me suspiciously. "I thought you only liked big dogs."

I shrugged. "There are exceptions to everything."

Sonya is in charge of casting *Just Friends*. I have to say that in other years she's always done a good job. Today was the day she was posting her choices. "So, who'd you end up picking?" I asked. We'd discussed it, of course, at the Playhouse 74 meeting, but Sonya had the final say.

"Audrey Sonde and Orson Ebert."

"Orson Ebert? You said you were going to pick Quinn Henderson!" Quinn Henderson has had most of the romantic leads in Hamilton plays and musicals. He's six feet tall, muscular with thick black hair and blue eyes. As Phil would say, Einstein doesn't turn over in his grave every time Quinn opens his mouth, but he has a certain unselfconscious presence on stage. Orson Ebert is Wolf's height, five feet six at most, and almost albino-looking with huge tortoiseshell glasses. He looks like he needs a blood transfusion. I am Mel Gibson crossed with Bruce Springsteen compared to Orson Ebert.

"Quinn's been in too many things," Sonya said imperturbably. "I wanted someone new."

"But Orson?"

"Look, Paul, this guy—I don't care what you *intended*—but in your play Jim acts like a real shithead to Marlene. And if you have a gorgeous hunk acting like that, every girl in the audience will hate him unequivocally. But if you have someone like Orson, who's sort of pathetic and unsure of himself, act that way, they'll think: 'Poor guy, he's really got problems. It's not his fault.' I'm letting you off the hook."

"Thanks a lot."

"I chose Audrey because she's lovely in a sensitive, not a bimboesque, way."

We were on the bus and a lady sitting across from us was listening with obvious amusement to our entire conversation. "If you want someone to go with Orson, why not Devona Balis?" I asked. Devona is a little chub with frizzy red-brown hair and a wide-eyed "What do I do now?" expression.

Sonya was staring glacially at a McDonald's ad. "I'm going by your portrayal. You've portrayed Marlene, née Fiona, as an intelligent, but, shall we say, troubled teenage girl. Audrey was wonderful in *The Bell Jar* and *Diary of Anne Frank*. Audiences respond to her."

"So, they'll end up seeing this as a play about a guy who's an ugly creep who seduces a sensitive feminist. I wonder where audience sympathy will lie. We should take a poll at the door."

Sonya let out a hoot. "Feminist! I've read the play eight times, in both versions. . . . Please, make my day, tell me in what way she's a feminist. She has no career ambitions. She babbles on incoherently about wanting to do 'something in medicine.' Every time the hero argues with her she sits there like a stuffed rabbit and doesn't even answer back. She—"

Once Sonya gets wound up, she can go on all day. "How

about *her* seducing him?'' I interrupted. ''Isn't that feminist? She doesn't take a passive role with men.''

''Apart from departures from real life which I won't go into,'' Sonya snapped, ''there is nothing feminist about, as Jim so kindly puts it, date-raping a drunken wimp. That's just the classic male thing of thinking women want to act as brutish and crude as men. We don't!''

I was hanging on to the bus strap and trying to keep my balance and not stare down the lady across the way, whose eyes were as wide as saucers. ''Then how do you explain—''

''If a man leads a woman on and she picks up on that and initiates what he is too ambivalent or terrified to initiate, that, in no court in the world, could be called date rape.'' We were at Hamilton. Sonya hurried off the bus.

I trailed beside her in silence. I was thinking of how Zoe had asked, ''Do you think I've been leading you on?'' Who does lead who on in any circumstances? Isn't it always both people in some strange unstructured dance? Zoe led me on because she perceived how I felt, I took extraordinary measures like buying her the book of love poems because of the way she looked at me over the cup of hot chocolate. It was strange, though. A year ago, an argument like this with Sonya would have wrecked my day. I'm not inarticulate, but Sonya and I somehow keep upping the ante until blood is flowing. Some of the time one of us apologizes, but blood is always drawn. I've never in my life had fights like that with anyone else. Wolf is like Phil, so genial and laid-back that you'd have to give him a set of instructions on how to fight dirty—and even then, it wouldn't work.

But this morning my body was encased in a magical protective shield which covered not only all my private parts, but my ego and heart as well. *Zoe loves me. Nothing else matters.* I saw Sonya, not as an argumentative bitch, but as a pathetic, angry, unfulfilled person. Wolf isn't making her happy in bed. If he was, we wouldn't have had that argument. She's a wounded soul. Of course, even I was not stupid enough to voice these sentiments aloud. I do value my life. But ever since that first night with Zoe, things don't get to me the way they used to. It would be like a multimillionaire bothering to stoop in the rain to pick up a penny.

I'm a wonderful lover. I've discovered my true talent in life. Not writing plays or making quick-witted verbal comebacks. It turns out my body, my dumb, useless, unjocklike body is great. It knows how to make Zoe happy. For that alone it could get into Yale on early admission. True, her only points of comparison are me and Paul—Paul versus Paul—but still. He is older, he's had more experience, and yet . . . She says there's no comparison, at least as far as sex goes.

Wolf, Annice, Sonya, and I are all in College Lit together. We've been reading *Women in Love*. I should've taken Modern Poetry, but this course has an interesting range of authors from Mary Shelley to Freud to Rousseau. Our teacher is Bart Thornby, an aging preppy guy who can be a pain sometimes, but whom I basically like.

"Some feminists," Thornby began, "have felt Lawrence went off the deep end with the sex scenes in this and, particularly, some of his later books like *Lady Chatterley's Lover*. . . . Have any of you read *Lady Chatterley's Lover* or *The Rainbow*?"

About half the class raised their hands.

"Well, how do you feel about that? I'd like to get a response from both sexes, please." The class is two-thirds girls, which is typical of most Hamilton lit classes.

Wolf raised his hand. He was sitting diagonally across from me, next to Sonya. "I think the sex scenes were really good," he said, looking embarrassed. "I mean, lyrical, but just . . . Like with Birkin and Ursula, they really . . . That scene where they go into the forest. They love each other, it's mutual. What's wrong with that?"

Shoot him down, Sonya. I looked at her. She was drawing in her notebook. She didn't say anything.

"I've never even had sex so maybe I shouldn't enter this discussion," Annice said. "But it did seem a little flowery to me. I mean, I'm sure sex is fun and all, but I don't get the woman melting into a puddle at the man's feet. I sure *hope* it isn't like that."

Annice has this peculiar bluntness combined with a funny kind of shyness. I doubt anyone else in class would have made such a personal reference. "They feel they're one person," I said, "and that that's for life. And I think Lawrence felt that was the most important thing, that everything else was based on that . . . for men too."

"But the men don't rave on about the women in the same way," Annice said.

"The book is called *Women in Love*," Thornby noted. "Why do you think that is? Why not *Men in Love*, or just *People in Love*?"

"I don't think he thought it was as big a deal to men," Annice said. "They just kind of do it and forget about it . . . somewhat. To women it's a big deal."

Thornby looked at me and Wolf who represent half the guys in the class other than Grant Lifshin who was absent and Ron Reiter who speaks one word every four months. "Okay guys? Want to speak for your sex? Or shall we let this pass?"

Wolf and I looked at each other and grinned. "I think it's a big deal for men," Wolf said. He looked warmly at Sonya.

"I do too," I agreed.

There was a pause.

Thornby looked at Sonya. "Ms. Niditch, how about giving us the distaff side? You've been rather quiet so far this session."

Sonya raised her head slowly. "I think it's a dumb book. What did Lawrence know? He was some little consumptive twerp married to a tank-like German countess who fucked around on the side. It was all in his head."

Thornby smiled. "Well, yes. . . . But with writers, I think a little of that is frequently the case."

"Writers should write what they know about," Sonya said fiercely, "not their fantasies."

"Possibly." Thornby is someone whom it is constitutionally impossible to rattle. "But I'm sure we oughtn't to dictate to the creative spirits among us, few as they are, about the sources of their inspiration."

In my mind all through class Zoe was lying there, naked, listening, not listening, just a presence, saying: *I'm real. You have a real life.*

That evening Phil came into my bedroom again. This time I was just reading a sci-fi novel Wolf had lent me. I'd done my homework. I looked up calmly. "Did you get the suit yet?" he asked.

"What suit?"

"For the wedding! My wedding's in two weeks."

"I have a suit."

"Show me. Get it out."

Phil stood there, arms akimbo, while I rummaged around in my closet and got out a dark blue suit he'd bought for me at Barney's about four years ago. Phil just looked at me. "Paulie, come on. Have you tried that on recently?"

I shook my head. I hate suits.

"The sleeves would come up to your elbows. I want you to do me proud. You'll look like a ragamuffin."

Sometimes I think Phil was a Jewish mother in another life.

"How about my tweed jacket?" That's the one I wore for my college interviews.

"Listen." Phil approached me. "I'm giving you three checks. You go to Brooks Brothers. You buy the nicest-looking suit you can find, regardless of price, and you have it sent. Maybe a few new shirts, too. Even a tie. You're going to be my best man. I want you to look snazzy."

I sighed. "I look ridiculous in suits."

"In a three-hundred-dollar Brooks Brothers suit you'll look sensational."

"But with that money I could buy—"

"With that money you're buying a suit, period. . . . Look, Paulie, how many times in my life, in your life, have I gotten married?"

"Never."

"This is it! Do you get what I mean? This is a big deal for me. I'm thirty-six years old. I'm not one of these guys who every ten years marries a new dame. This is for *life*."

That sounded scary. "How can you tell?"

"When it happens to you, you'll know. You just feel it—in your bones, in your head. . . . So do me a favor. Look terrific, okay?"

I folded up the checks. "Okay." I smiled.

"You'll have a good suit. Unless you grow another foot, you'll have it—for college, for dances. Why not?"

After Phil left I lay staring at the ceiling. It's not just that I hate suits. I also hate weddings. Why couldn't Phil elope? They're both in their thirties. What good does it do to stand up in front of some idiot rabbi and have him mutter some nonsense? Of course, it's Jayne's first marriage. All her relatives will be there. At least Penny and Mike did it when I was just a kid. Pen says I carried the ring in a little blue velvet box, but I have total amnesia about the whole event. I'm not a suit type. I'm not going to end up as some slick yuppie in a vest working on Madison Avenue. I look like a monkey in a suit. I look unnatural. For three hundred dollars I could buy every record or book I've wanted for ages. But I have no choice. Phil wants me in a suit. He's right. Probably it is for life. They'll bury me in that suit. It's the last one I'll ever buy.

The next morning, as I was lying in bed with Zoe, looking at her digital clock which read 8:05, I told her about having to get a suit. I love these mornings with Zoe. It's just one hour, usually, and of course making love to her is the high point. But I like all the rest too. I like hearing about her sister in Ohio who has a bad back and can't decide if she should go back into nursing or about the horse they had that Zoe used to ride when she was in junior high and who's ready to cave in. I tell her all about me too, dumb little things from my childhood, about the time Wolf and I went out for Halloween both dressed as the hero of *A Clockwork Orange*, and no one knew who we were, or the time I ran into Cindy in her nightgown coming into our bathroom. Just making love wouldn't be the same. It's the combination, that they flow together, that we can say anything and no one gets mad or takes anything the wrong way. The only thing we never talk about is her husband. We talk around him sometime, but we never discuss him directly. Zoe'll say, "We have go to a party tonight," and then describe the party. But I'm glad. I don't want to talk about him. He doesn't exist for me. Why should I spend my time thinking about him? I could feel jealous, but she says that when they make love, she pretends he's me. What's there to feel jealous about?

"You *should* get a suit," Zoe said. She was lying on her stomach. I love that line of her back dipping into her ass which is so beautifully small and rounded. "Gray, maybe. You'd look very distinguished in gray."

"He wants me to go to Brooks Brothers," I said gloomily. "I hate men's stores with all those obsequious little sales-people."

"But they have beautiful suits," Zoe said. "How about if I go with you?"

"How can you? I'm going on Saturday!"

"I'll come with you. I have to do some Christmas shopping anyway. They have a women's department too, you know."

How does she know? Has she gone there with him?

"Do you not want me to?" Zoe said, picking up on the mixed expression on my face. "You go alone, then." She turned aside with a little pout.

"Zoe, I'd love you to go. . . . But it'll be dull. I'll just be trying on suits. It might take hours. I look unbelievably awful in suits. You just don't know."

"You said you hadn't bought one in four years." Zoe reached over and hugged me. "It'll be so much fun! What time should we meet?"

We arranged to meet at two in front of Brooks Brothers. I guess Zoe doesn't know that many people in New York she's afraid of running into and I certainly don't. Somehow, walking into Brooks Brothers with Zoe next to me was a completely different experience. She was in a red coat with a black fur collar. She looked bright-eyed and beautiful and it seemed to me we could have been lovers or boyfriend-and-girlfriend. We didn't look ill-matched at all as a couple. A lot better matched than she and her stupid husband any day.

I couldn't believe the prices on the suits. "Paul, stop looking at the prices," she said. "Phil said buy whatever you want. These are good values. The tailoring is excellent. How about this one?''

She'd picked out a charcoal-gray three-piece suit that looked as though it should be worn by some banker of about fifty. "Can you really see me in that?''

"Sure, you'd look super. Try it on.''

"It's the wrong size.''

"Find it in the right size.''

At this point a tiny bespectacled salesman had attached himself to us. "We have another suit in very much the same style without the vest," he said.

"Great, I hate vests," I said.

Zoe had taken off her coat. Underneath she was wearing a bright pink dress. She was far and away the prettiest woman in the store. "This is for a wedding," she explained to the salesman. "But we want something that will be useful for other occasions.''

"Of course. . . . But gray is perfect for a wedding. And yet, when you go out, to the theater or dancing, it is also perfect.''

"Try it on, Paul," Zoe said. "I think he's right. Gray is the perfect color.''

Amazingly, the jacket fit me. It was a 40 long. The pants were a little short. I looked at myself and then went out of the dressing room. Zoe beamed. "Wow, you look gorgeous! It's fantastic.''

"The pants are a little short," the salesman mumbled. "Let's find a longer pair." He wandered off.

I went over to Zoe. "You really think I look fantastic?'' I said uncertainly. I did look better than I'd expected.

"Look at yourself!" she dragged me over to the three-way mirror. "You could get a job anywhere in that suit. It's so . . . it's perfect.''

I stared at myself. All I saw was a gangling guy with frizzy hair who looked like he was going to a funeral. But with Zoe next to me, her eyes sparkling with admiration, I also saw another person: sophisticated, dapper, suave. I saw us going to the theater. A first night. My first play.

I tried on a few more suits of a similar type, but in the end

I got the gray one. Then, carried away, I got three shirts and a tie. I was beginning to feel heady, whipping out Phil's checks. Then I got a brainstorm. "Let's get something for you," I said.

"The ladies' department is on four," the salesman said. He was ready to pick out our trousseau and send us around the world.

"What will it be for?" Zoe asked.

"Because you're beautiful," I whispered. "Because I'm so lucky. Because I want to."

She blushed. "Just something small. . . . It's Phil's money, remember."

But I knew Phil would approve. This time I stood and waited while Zoe tried on a bunch of silk blouses. We decided on one in turquoise blue. With her pale skin and black hair she looked exquisite. "Would you like it gift-wrapped?" the saleswoman asked.

"No, just put it in a box," Zoe said. I knew she was thinking of how to explain it to Paul.

"Tell him it's from an unknown admirer," I said with a sly grin.

She frowned and then smiled. She reached up and kissed me. "It's a beautiful blouse, Paul. Thanks so much."

For some reason I started wondering if Zoe usually went shopping with her husband. For him this wouldn't even be a lot of money. He probably has ten suits like this. So what? He's still chubby and graying and looks like a shlump. Does Zoe stare at him that way with that sparkle? I felt like every man in the store was envying me. We walked out into the bright December sunshine. "Let's have hot chocolate," Zoe said.

We did. We found a bar that had something called Lover's Chocolate, hot chocolate with Amaretto. "I guess there can't be many days like this in anyone's life," Zoe said, gazing at me pensively. Zoe says she hates to act, that she's much too shy and self-conscious; but if I were a movie director, I'd make a whole movie of close-ups of her face. The way her skin changes color. It's so pale, almost white normally, but on a cold day she gets red cheeks just like a girl ice-skating in a Dutch painting. And now, she still had that sparkle, but it was subdued, with a glaze of sadness in her eyes and the set of her mouth. *Don't be sad, you're with me.*

"Why should there be only a few?" I said, knowing what she meant. "Maybe, if you're with the right person, every day can be like this."

She shook her head. "I don't think so."

"You don't think being with the right person matters?"

Zoe smiled and reached out to touch my hand. "Yes, I do think it matters."

The waiter brought our hot chocolate. They'd poured in a gigantic dollop of Amaretto. "Hey, this is great," I said, after the first gulp.

"We're going to get looped," Zoe said. "I can't hold liquor."

"So? We're celebrating! My first and last suit. Phil's getting married, my play being put on—"

"My getting an A on my paper on Arthur Miller," Zoe slipped in.

"You did? You didn't even mention it."

She looked delighted. "The teacher said it was the best in the class. He said I was the only one who didn't take a completely uncritical, reverential attitude to his work."

We clinked our mugs of hot chocolate. "And Paul's opening a new store in White Plains," she continued, "and my sister thinks she may have a job—"

I set my mug down angrily. "I'm not drinking to your husband's fucking store in White Plains! He's filthy rich already. The world has enough orthopedic shoes. Let people go barefoot!"

"Paul, don't be childish. . . . First, we're not filthy rich. We're comfortably middle-class, at best. And Paul does this because he loves it. He happens to be a good businessman the way you're a good playwright. Not everyone can be creative."

I try not to do this, but I hate Zoe even to mention her husband, especially when she tries in this pathetic way to defend him and his gross, materialistic values. "So, what are you going to do with the money? Take a trip around the world?''

"We're just going to invest it." Zoe looked annoyed. "I never even ask you about girls at Hamilton, girls you may be—''

"Oh, come on. There *are* no girls at Hamilton."

She looked surprised. "I thought you said it was coed."

"It is, but all I get from Sonya are feminist harangues. You actually have sex with this guy."

" 'This guy,' '' Zoe said coldly, "is someone I'm *married* to.''

We were both getting angry—our first major fight. "Whose mistake was that?" I fired back.

Zoe turned pale. "It was no one's mistake."

We sat in silence, miserable. I'd drunk my hot chocolate quickly and my body seemed to be giving off heat. I hate apologizing, even when I'm wrong, but I also hated seeing Zoe look so miserable and I knew I'd been acting like a brat. "I'm sorry. I'm a jerk. . . . Let's go back and make love."

"How can we?" Zoe said. "Paul's at home."

"We can go to Phil's. He spends weekends at Jayne's."

"But that's right in our building. What if—"

I was already excited. In my mind we were there, our clothes strewn around the room. "It takes two seconds to cross the lobby. If you like, I'll go first and you can come up two minutes later. Pablo doesn't give a damn. He's just there to screen strangers."

"It seems dangerous," Zoe said, looking tempted.

"That'll make it more exciting." Maybe it's that innocent quality Zoe still has, having grown up on a farm, but I never feel she's older than me. A lot of times I feel as though she's younger.

She gulped down her cocoa, we paid, and I masterfully hailed a cab. It was one of those days when I knew that I could just walk out on Madison Avenue and Forty-fourth and get a cab immediately. Even the tips of my fingers were magical.

Zoe said she'd wait two minutes in front of our building. I raced upstairs. Oh no, my room was a mess. I hurled everything into the closet—books, papers, dirty clothes—and made the bed. Just as I was finishing, the doorbell rang. I ran to open the door. Zoe was smiling. "Is this the Gold residence?"

"You bet."

I took her coat and hung it in the closet, the same closet where I'd crouched furtively that night, listening to her voice on the phone telling me she'd liked the presents. I told her about that. Zoe looked up at me. "You've had such a different childhood from me. My parents were there all the time, every *second*. You come and go. Phil spends weekends with Jayne. . . . I've never in my whole *life* had that much freedom, that much independence. I didn't when I was living at home, and now—" She broke off, obviously not wanting to get into the subject of her marriage again. "Show me around."

I did. She looked inquisitively around. "It's comfortable, lived-in," she said, diplomatically, obviously comparing it mentally to their place.

"Phil doesn't have much cash. He inherited this from his grandmother. He's probably paying a quarter of what you are for the same amount of space."

"I'm sure." She looked up at me shyly. "So, where do we go?"

I showed her my room. "Voilà!"

Zoe hesitated. "Is this where you and Sonya—"

"No, we used Phil's bed. *This* is a virgin bed." I sat down on it. "Feel it. Pure, white, firm."

Zoe looked at it suspiciously. "It's so narrow."

"Not for one person." I was getting undressed and so was she, but she was doing it much more slowly. I didn't know if she was still hesitant because of the relative physical proximity of her husband. "Is anything wrong?"

She looked at me and then out the window. "Well, it's just I'm at the tail end of my period."

"So?"

"Paul hates to do it, even then. Something about the blood."

"Is he an Orthodox Jew?"

"No, it's just . . . I guess the smell, or maybe the idea. I just wanted you to know."

I went over and embraced her. "Everything about you smells wonderful. I couldn't care less, if you don't."

Thank you, oh Lord, for making her husband such a consummate fool. I kissed Zoe everywhere, even between her legs and there was no smell except her usual warm, intoxicating female scent. I used to think doing that to a woman would be sickening, but to do it to Zoe while she lies there in a trance of pleasure, murmuring my name, is the greatest high on earth. When we made love, she was moister than usual, but I didn't care. If anything, it was a kind of double turn-on, doing something to her that no person had ever done before. When I withdrew, a spurt of bright red blood came out on the sheet. There was a slight trace of blood on my penis.

"Oh no," Zoe cried in alarm. "Look at the sheet! What'll Phil say?"

"Phil never even comes in here. I do my own laundry in the basement. I have since I was ten. . . . Anyway, I'm not going to wash this. I'm going to save it as a memento."

There was some blood smudged between Zoe's legs. I brought her a wet towel and she wiped it off. "I don't even mind getting my period," she said. "Maybe because I don't get terrible cramps the way some women do. It's just—"

"Just what?"

"Well, it reminds me again that I'm not pregnant and that Paul—"

"You're not a brood mare. If he wanted one, he should have married one."

"Don't you want children once you're married?"

"First, I may not even get married, but definitely not till I'm in my mid-thirties at least."

"And your wife?" Zoe asked shyly.

"What wife?" I looked at her teasingly. We were lying pressed close together on the bed.

"The person you're going to marry . . . How old will she be? Your age?"

"Yeah, sure. . . . Or maybe ten years older like Jayne's brother's wife. I don't care."

Zoe looked at me with her caressing glance. "It's all so remote for you, something that'll happen in a million years."

"Not at all. It could happen next year. . . . I just don't have any set plan. I want to enjoy life, I want whoever I marry to enjoy her life. I don't think of marriage as two people chained together, trudging side by side into eternity."

Sighing, Zoe rolled over on her back, staring at the ceiling.

"I wish you'd gone to Hamilton," I said suddenly. "I wish I'd met you before you met Paul."

She laughed bitterly. "I never would have gotten in, not in a million years. I'm not like your friends, Paul. I'm not a 'highly gifted' whatever. I'm just an ordinary person."

"You got an A on your drama report," I reminded her.

"Probably because the teacher has the hots for me."

I was horrified. She hadn't even said the teacher was male. "Who is he? Is he married?"

"Yeah, he's in his forties and into his second marriage. Don't get all excited. I just said that because he stares at me in a certain way when we have conferences. That's probably the way he stares at all the female students, hoping one will—"

"Drop the course!" I yelled. "He sounds terrible."

Zoe rubbed her nose against my bellybutton. "Paul, calm down. It's a good course. I'm learning a lot. I was just joking before."

But it was true. I'd thought of this as just a contest between two Pauls. In fact, there Zoe was, out in New York City with thousands of horny guys seeing her on the street, following her into doorways, pretending to like her insights into Arthur Miller. "The world is a dangerous place," I said darkly.

"But here we're safe," Zoe said, kissing me.

I love it when Zoe says things like that, unexpectedly, out of the blue. *Here we're safe.* And several hundred feet away Paul Bernstein is—what?—watching TV? Snoozing while waiting for his wife to come home from doing her Christmas shopping? We fell asleep as the afternoon darkened around us, but Zoe was right. It felt safe, warm, comfortable, like two animals snuggled into their private lair. No one can harm us here. The world is at bay.

CHAPTER 12

Today, the day before Christmas vacation started, we had a read-through on *Just Friends*. Wolf is directing it. He's not the most forceful director, but he's good with someone like Audrey who is almost scarily ethereal. Toward the end he said, "Aud, I like the way you're doing it. I think you've caught Marlene's intensity, her frightening quality. . . . But I think it needs maybe a little more sensuality. She doesn't go to bed with Jim just because she gets drunk. She's really attracted to him."

Thanks, Wolf. I was sitting to one side, just listening. Whatever I felt, I could tell Wolf some other time. I didn't want to interfere in front of the actors.

"I don't see it that way," Audrey said. "I think she just wanted to lose her virginity and Jim was the lucky—or unlucky—target."

Sonya was absent that day, but her presence hovered over us. "That doesn't square with how I read the play," Wolf said. "How about her bitterness at the end, her feeling of hurt when he says, 'I don't love you.' "

"Well, everyone feels that way if someone says that,"

Audrey said. "Of *course* she wants him to love her. . . . I see Marlene as someone who likes control. She wants to use Jim, but when it ends up that, in a way, *he* was using *her*, she gets mad. But it kind of serves her right."

Wow. Thank God Sonya isn't here. Thank God I *am* here. Audrey, I love you. "Perfect," was all I said.

Wolf shot me a warning glance. "Is that how *you* see it, Orson? You're reading it much more as though Jim *is* in love with Marlene so I think the audience is going to be kind of shocked at the end when he says he isn't."

Orson bit off a hangnail. "Well, I agree with Marlene's interpretation, I mean Audrey's interpretation of Marlene. But I think Jim *is* kind of in love with her, or in lust with her. I mean, how do people really know, ever? . . . But he's also an honest guy. He wasn't using her, but he doesn't feel ready for a full-blown romantic whatever. Do you get what I mean?"

"I do," Wolf said. "I think that's good. . . . What I think we need to move toward is maybe warming up Marlene and cooling down Paul, I mean Jim." He laughed nervously. "We've had all these name changes. Sometimes I forget."

Audrey looked over at me. "I didn't get why you changed her name from Fiona to Marlene," she said. "Fiona's so much prettier. She sounds more like a Fiona to me."

"Well, let's leave it at Marlene," Wolf said quickly. "Names aren't that crucial. . . . The point is, we want both Marlene and Jim to be sympathetic, but mixed-up. They really don't *know* what they want—or they want two contradictory things. Marlene *seems* hot-headed and aggressive, but deep down she's insecure and gentle. You bring out the gentleness nicely, Aud. . . . And Jim is hitting the ball back into her court. His pretending she's seducing him is part of his self-image, a kind of protection."

I think I'm gong to be a bricklayer. Or maybe a sales manager like Phil. Here they are, sitting discussing my fucking soul like it was a bag of dried potato flakes! Maybe it is.

After everyone cleared out, I said to Wolf, "Thanks."

"I hate having you here," he said. "Thank God Sonya wasn't."

"I didn't say a word . . . almost."

"Yeah, but you . . . See, I like you *and* Son. And you both have a case. And yet I feel like I should be directing the play, not arbitrating a single fuck that took place months ago."

"Many fucks under the bridge," I said jocularly.

"Under *whose* bridge?" Wolf bantered back. "I thought you said that girl—"

I hesitated. If it was a girl at Hamilton, if it was anyone but Zoe . . . But I knew I couldn't. "It was an inept metaphor," I said.

"I wish your play was about the discovery of bubble gum," Wolf said.

"My next one will be. . . . You didn't have to direct this, you know."

"I wanted to. . . . I just think it makes lung transplants look like a piece of cake."

"Yuck. . . . Talk about inept metaphors."

We walked out of the building together. "What's wrong with Sonya?" I said. "I mean, why wasn't she at rehearsal?"

"She has her period. She gets horrible cramps."

I thought of the bloodstained sheet. I had washed it after all. Suddenly I said, "Something *is* happening in my life, but I can't tell you about it."

Wolf looked surprised. "When can you tell me?"

"I don't know."

"Is it serious?"

"Yeah."

We walked in silence to the bus stop. The reason I will always cherish Wolf, to the end of my days, is that he can listen and know when to *not* ask questions.

"Phil's getting married next week," I said. "I'm going to be his best man."

"Good for him," Wolf said genially. "About time."

Phil and Jayne got married in the living room of her parents. They live in Teaneck, New Jersey, in a nice, typical, expensive-looking suburban home, wall-to-wall carpets. What Penny and Mike would have if they could afford it.

What I would pay never to have. Jayne's father has a collection of digital recordings, all filed by name of composer—he's evidently an opera buff. Her mother weaves and her little tasteful hangings were draped here and there on the wall. I don't know how delighted they were about Phil, but I'm sure all those discussions took place behind closed doors. Now all was forced good fellowship. There were about fifty people, but most of them were older, relatives, friends of Jayne's parents. I guess Phil was right about my suit. It looked like I'd just escaped from Harvard Business School. Still, since Zoe helped me buy the suit, it had a kind of special feeling for me.

"You're Phil's son?" Mrs. Shivers asked me. She was a tall woman, like Jayne, with dyed dark-brown hair and an air of dignity. She had a gold-encrusted choker around her neck with small green jewels in it. "It's amazing. You're so grown-up!"

"Well, I'm eighteen," I said. "Eighteen isn't that young."

"I suppose it's that I can scarcely imagine Phil with a son that age, he seems so young himself . . . in a good way, I mean. So full of life and enthusiasm. Most of us have that squeezed out along the way."

"Yeah, well, Phil's a good guy. He's a good father too." Why was I acting so phony? I was acting the way I thought she wanted me to.

"You seem more like friends than father and son. . . . Goodness, my father would have bitten my head off if I'd called him by his first name. Of course that was many eons ago, way back in the days of the dinosaurs." She looked around as her husband approached. "Dear, I was just telling Paul how wonderful I think it is that he and Phil have managed to be friends all these years, despite being father and son. Imagine being friends with our parents!"

Mr. Shivers frowned. "But how about role models? How about regarding one's parents with respect? . . . I think that's all nonsense. Parents aren't meant to be friends. They're meant to be parents, damn it!"

Wow, I love guys like this. How did Jayne turn out so nice? "Oh, Phil's been a great role model," I said heartily. "I don't think what you call someone determines what you feel about them."

"And you lived with who?" Mrs. Shivers intervened, before her husband could go into another harangue.

"Well, back and forth, really. . . . When I was a baby, mostly with Penny, my mother, and my grandmother, Rose. Then, once Pen got married and had more kids, I stayed mostly with Phil."

Mr. Shivers's face darkened again. "Who's Penny?"

Mrs. Shivers took his arm and patted it. "Dear, you know. . . . Phil was married before, to a lovely young Catholic girl named Penny. That's Paul's mother."

From the look on Shivers's face this was the first he'd heard of it. "A *Catholic* girl? What'd he do a damn fool thing like that for?"

"Dear!" Mrs. Shivers gasped. "Penny is Paul's *mother*, and evidently an excellent one. She went back to school, finished her education, has remarried, and—"

"Fooling around is one thing," Mr. Shivers said. "*I* fooled around too, we *all* fooled around. . . . But marrying them!"

I was really getting riled. "They were in love," I said. I hoped he didn't know about Penny's pregnancy.

"Love!" Mr. Shivers snorted.

"Love makes the world go round," trilled Mrs. Shivers gaily. "Just look at Phil and Jayne. Doesn't she look radiant! I've never *seen* her so happy!"

"Then where's that damn rabbi?" Mr. Shivers snarled. "We can't stand around all day."

"I think he may have just arrived," Mrs. Shivers said. "I'll be back in a sec."

Mr. Shivers and I were left locked in eye-to-eye combat. "So, you going into business like your father?"

"No, I'm going to be a playwright."

He looked uneasy. "Plays? No one goes to plays anymore. Write for the movies. That's where the money is."

I thought of how when I was eight I used to imagine pressing an imaginary button and having people I hated disappear into pale gray smoke before my very eyes. "I'm not interested in money," I said stiffly.

117

"So, what are you interested in?"

"Language, art, expressing what I feel about the world." I knew I was sounding like as big an ass as he was, in my own way.

Surprisingly, Mr. Shivers laughed. He slapped me on the shoulder. "Just be sure to marry a rich wife, okay? Promise?"

Mercifully at that moment the rabbi announced that the ceremony was about to begin. I can never listen to rabbis for more than three seconds without either going to sleep or feeling what Mr. Shivers was probably feeling while I babbled on about writing. But I thought instead how many times in my life I've had variations on that conversation. Why does everyone in the world care that much that everyone else do things their way?

After the ceremony everyone had champagne and I stood on a receiving line and said what I assumed I was supposed to say. People admired my suit, exclaimed at how tall I was, were awed that Phil had a son already almost in college. I gathered Phil had told them about *Just Friends* being put on at Hamilton and a lot of them had gotten that mixed up and thought I was having a real play put on on Broadway or Off Broadway. Since most of my conversations lasted an average of two minutes, I didn't correct everyone. To one very pretty cousin I just said yes, it was a tremendous thrill. To someone else I said yes, I was nervous about reviews, but thought the cast was doing a fine job. I heard one person whisper to another, "He's just eighteen!" Boy genius.

Phil wasn't nervous anymore, just euphoric. He and Jayne kissed for the official photographer, a tiny man with beady eyes who looked a little like Peter Lorre.

The Shivers had treated Phil and Jayne to a four-day honeymoon in the Caribbean. When the partying was in full swing, they snuck out the back. Phil gave me a hug. "Take care," he whispered.

"Have fun," I said. What are you supposed to say to your father as he goes off on his honeymoon? If he doesn't know how to have fun at thirty-six, he's pretty hopeless. Of course they'd have fun. They must have a decent sex life. Sex is important to Phil. He's never treated me to any long discussions on the topic, but I gather he puts it fairly high up on the list of things that count. I guess I would too, now. Five months ago I would have assumed it was something that just happened naturally if you loved someone. But maybe just the way Wolf and I have had a kind of rapport ever since we were throwing sand at each other in the playground, maybe that kind of physical rapport, that I have with Zoe, is just as rare. Shit. I know Zoe envisions our relationship as a brief, crazy, intense fling that will end with my going off to college. I do too, but at the same time, parallel to that, I imagine it never ending. I could be The Other Man. Maybe we could do this for the next ten years till I was ready to really get married and at that point she could pass me on to someone else, like the heroine of *Der Rosenkavalier*. Or maybe Paul Bernstein will just drop dead without warning. You hear about that all the time. I'll let him live till he's forty. That seems only fair. And then Zoe and I . . .

Someone drove me home, some couple the Shivers' age who lived in Manhattan. I sat in the backseat and pretended to fall asleep. Sometimes I do that just to overhear people's conversations, but this time I really did sleep and they had to wake me up when I got to Phil's building. It was five-twenty, Saturday. People were dragging Christmas trees into the lobby. In fact, as I entered the building, as ill luck would have it, I saw Zoe and her husband tipping Pablo as he helped them load a small tree onto the back elevator. Zoe didn't see me. I hurried past, filled with such a wave of anger and despair I wasn't sure I'd make it across the lobby.

What's wrong with you? What do you expect her to be doing on Saturday? What's so unusual about buying a Christmas tree? But they looked so normal, so much like a couple. I envisioned Zoe making hot chocolate and the two of them trimming the tree together and then . . . Of course they'll make love. Or maybe they already have. I know their erotic schedule by heart. It's every Saturday, and sometimes, "if Paul is up to it," Sundays too, usually after lunch. It takes about three minutes and then they both take a nap. That's it, for him anyway, till the following week. He's tired during the week, Zoe explains. All those earth-shaking decisions about the design and manufacture of orthopedic shoes wear a guy out. And he's a big deal, though Zoe never puts it quite that way. He fires people who aren't doing their job or he agonizes and decides to give them a second chance. And then he has to hire new people. . . . So, of course, who has time during the week to do something as exhausting as making love? Look, what are you depressed about. You're *glad* he's like that.

But weekends depress me now. Maybe they always did. Maybe it does go back to my childhood. Weekends were never what they were in books, jolly family times. They were times when Penny had to work or shop or study or Phil was off with some new conquest. And now it's two days when I lie around thinking of Zoe and her husband snuggled together in *his* bed. So she's thinking of me? Who cares. Maybe she just says that. Maybe she's thinking of Sting or Mel Gibson.

Sunday at the bookstore, the day after the wedding, my mood lifted a little. Sunday is the bookstore's busiest day. A lot of artsy-looking young couples come in after lunch and browse around, some gallery-goers. It can get pretty hectic. Sometimes people ask my advice on what to buy and I tell them. Usually they just thrust some book or pile of magazines at me and I ring it up or run it through the American Express machine. In the middle of the afternoon, a girl asked me if I could give her some advice about a book of poetry. "It's for my cousin," she said. "She's getting married. I thought maybe a book of love poetry. I know that's sort of corny, but they're getting married on Valentine's Day."

She looked to be my age or maybe in college, thick brown straight hair, red-rimmed eyeglasses, and a kind of mischievous, merry expression around her mouth. I saw that the store had one more copy of the book I'd given Zoe for her birthday. "This is a little expensive," I said, "but it's really beautifully printed and it's an unusual selection. I think it's the best we have."

She leafed through it and hit on that e.e. cummings poem which is right in the middle. " 'i like my body when it is with your body,' " she read aloud. She blushed and looked up at me. "Wow. . . . Anna is a little straight-laced. I guess I was thinking of something more romantic."

"This has romantic ones, too," I said. I was flirting with her, consciously, but it seemed to me she was flirting back. "Anyhow, you said she's getting married so maybe it's about time she learned the facts of life."

The girl laughed. "Let's hope so. . . . Okay, I'll take it. Could you wrap it?"

As fate would have it, it was ten, the end of my working day. As I handed the book to her, I grabbed my coat and walked out of the store. She looked up, puzzled. "I just work here two days a week," I said. "I'm really a student."

"Oh, me too. . . . Where?"

"Hamilton." I was sure she was in college which turned out to be the case. If you just say "Hamilton" most people assume you mean the college. Her name was Donna. On the way to the coffee shop—there are about a hundred within a one-block radius of the store—I wondered what I was doing and why—a bad habit of mine. Let it happen, as someone has no doubt said. Revenge on Zoe? For what? For being married? Look, a pretty girl passed your way and you're having coffee with her. Even in the sixteenth century they didn't hang people for that.

Donna was from a suburb of L.A. "But not the typical thing. My parents grew up in Brooklyn. They hate it out there but it's where my dad got a job. They'd sell their souls to be where I am now. . . . I really lucked out, getting into NYU, getting an apartment."

I was drinking cappuccino. I dumped in a couple of packets of sugar. "How'd you get an apartment?" I said. "There aren't any for under a million dollars."

"I know! . . . But my sister's old roommate sublet it to me. She's in London for the year. It's just two blocks from here, Eight Bleecker. I can walk to classes. It's so perfect, every time I go back there I'm afraid it'll have vanished."

I don't know what it was, just my personality or Phil's wedding or it being Sunday and some peripheral sadness still clinging to me, but I saw Donna's apartment, I saw us entering it, taking our clothes off, making love, lying there, talking, my leaving. She was describing the courses she was taking and I was mentally making it with her and thinking, "Why not? Why *not* have a one-night stand?" She hadn't exactly asked me, yet if a girl begins talking about her apartment and even telling you the address after five minutes, I think you don't need a doctorate in psychology to feel it means something. Obviously I was, by New York City standards, clean-cut, literary, a "good listener."

But I couldn't. I didn't even want to, or anyway, not enough. I didn't want to dilute what I had with Zoe with some random, probably pleasant screw. Donna seemed like a nice girl. Not that I'm vain enough to think anyone will fall in love with me the minute they gaze upon my incomparable body, but I had the feeling there would be sticky (no pun) moments as I left and that she'd straggle into the bookstore some weeks later and I'd feel guilty and rotten. "I'm just in high school," I said, just to strip some of the rosy veiling from my identity. "It's Hamilton High School."

"Oh, you're just in high school," Donna said. "You look older."

Maybe being with Zoe has made me seem older. I told Donna about how I got the job and my wanting to write and about Phil's getting married. "I hope he has a good honeymoon," I said, still flirting a bit.

Donna clinked her cappuccino cup with mine. "How can you *not* have a good honeymoon?"

I laughed. "I don't know. . . . I've never been on one."

I walked her home and at the door she asked if I felt like coming up. I told her that I had to get home to study, and it was cool. I didn't feel like I'd even slightly broken her heart. By now it was Sunday night. The next morning I would be in bed with Zoe. I had survived another weekend.

CHAPTER 13

For some reason I never worried, when I was in bed with Zoe, that her husband might return unexpectedly. I gave myself over to the moment and even his existence became unimportant. But that Monday, the day after the day after Phil's wedding, the doorbell rang when we were right in the middle of doing it. We froze.

"It couldn't be Paul," Zoe whispered. "He has a key."

"Maybe he forgot it."

"He never forgets things." We disengaged. She pulled on her underpants and her nightgown and bathrobe and rushed out to the front hall. I heard her say, "Who is it?" Even though we have a doorman in our building, no one who values their life opens their door to a stranger. Then I heard the door open. Zoe said, "Oh hi, Pablo. . . . Yes, that's right, the light in the bathroom. It does need fixing. It's just that now isn't such a good time. Is there a chance you could come back later? . . . Right. That would be great."

The door closed again. I realized I was still lying there, as though I'd been flung in a game of statues, naked on the bed. Why? What if it *had* been her husband? Zoe's expression when she returned and saw me that way was aghast. "Paul, my God! You're just lying there!"

"So?"

"But what if it—"

"It was Pablo."

"But what if it hadn't been? Don't you care?" She seemed slightly hysterical.

"Of course I care. . . . What should I have done? Hidden in the closet?"

Zoe sat down next to me. I still, perhaps due to inertia, had an erection. She looked at it dispassionately, like an object someone had forgotten to put away. "This is all so different for you, just some fling, some little . . . I would die if Paul found out! I'm not blaming myself or you or anyone, but there's no reason *he* should suffer. He's a good person. He hasn't done any harm to anyone."

I felt irritated, sulky. "He's not going to find out. . . . I'm certainly not telling him."

"Are you telling anyone?"

"No!"

"Not even Wolf?"

"Of course not! Christ, Zoe, what do you think I am?"

She sighed. "I've just heard men always—"

"Men always, women always . . . Who cares about some stupid clichés that someone thought up a thousand years ago? This isn't a fling. What kind of insult is that? Do you think I'm just some horny high-school kid who couldn't get laid and took the first offer that came his way?"

Zoe took off the bathrobe and lay down, still in her nightgown, on the bed. "I don't know."

"God, I really feel wonderful now," I said bitterly. "This is a super way to start the week."

She looked listlessly at the digital clock. "You should start getting dressed and go to school."

I pointed ironically to my erection. "What should I do about this?"

"It'll go away eventually, won't it?" But she laughed.

I reached over and began kissing her. Zoe half-struggled.

"Paul, don't. We don't have time. I'm not in the mood anymore. I felt so scared."

"Don't be scared." I kept kissing her. "No one knows. No one will ever know."

She allowed me to pull her nightgown off and pull down her underpants. "You'll be late for school."

We didn't bother finishing that argument. Somehow, maybe it was the excitement of having been interrupted, or our partial quarrel, I felt more excited than usual, less able to go slowly, the way Zoe likes. I came in a minute or two. I could tell she hadn't. "Do you want me to go on?" I whispered.

"Would you mind?"

Somehow it was as though the incident with Pablo had affected us differently. For me it had been a turn-on. For Zoe it had been a turn-off. It wasn't until quite a while after I stayed in her, even after my erection was gone, that she finally came with a series of small muffled cries. She smiled as I withdrew. "Was that awful, having to wait for hours while I—"

"No. . . . And it wasn't hours. Minutes maybe. Can you still enjoy it? There wasn't much left of me."

"I still can. . . . It's just so hard for me to stop worrying! But finally I did." She smiled at me with her usual tender expression. "You're going to be late for school! And it's snowing out."

"Maybe I'll skip school today." I lay back, staring at the ceiling.

"Paul, you can't. You can't just skip school."

"Why not? Kids do it all the time."

"But you're not the type. . . . And if you do it once, you might—"

"End up a Bowery bum? And when they find me, drunk and ragged, leaning on a trash can and say, 'How did this all begin?' I'll say, 'It was a snowy morning in January and . . .' "

Zoe was looking worried again. "What will you do with the day?"

I grinned.

"I can't. We can't spend the day in bed! I have a paper to type for my Psych course, I have an exam in Poetry tomorrow, we're having guests for dinner, Paul's new sales manager and his wife are coming and I have to—"

I raised my hand. "Stop! How's this? We'll just spend the day together. You can study, I'll study. I'll help you with your cooking."

She sighed. "You know that's not going to work."

"Scout's honor. . . . Have you started your paper yet?"

"I've written it, but I have to go over it and type it and my typewriter needs a new ribbon."

I sat up. "Okay, here's the plan. We stay here till noon. . . . Then we go over to Phil's and I type your paper on my computer while you study for your poetry exam."

"Would you really?" Zoe looked delighted. "I'm such a terrible typist. And I'm slow."

"I'm incredible. Fast *and* accurate. It'll look so good you won't believe it."

Zoe lay back and snuggled against me. "It *is* fun playing hooky from school, isn't it? I only did it a couple of times, with my friend Alice. We never did anything special, but it was the *idea*. Especially with the snow."

We made love once more. I felt like we were inside one of those crystal balls with artificial snow drifting down on us, warm, enclosed. Afterward, when I went down to walk Baby, it was still snowing, big soft moist flakes of snow. I hate winter, but this was the kind of snow you knew would disappear by nightfall. Even as the flakes hit the ground, they were melting. The thought of the entire day with Zoe lay in front of me like an incredible gift that someone had bought for me, wonderful because unexpected.

For the rest of the morning Zoe did some housework and fixed the main course for the dinner party she was giving. I read *Jane Eyre* and when I'd finished the chapters that I was supposed to read by tomorrow, went into the kitchen to watch her cook. She was very nervous about it. I got a kick out of sitting on a stool and watching her. She even had an apron on, over her jeans and sweater. "It says soak prunes in tea for half an hour," she said, as though to herself. "Why tea?"

I laughed. "You're asking me? My cooking repertoire extends from hamburgers to fried chicken and then comes to an abrupt stop. Just skip the tea and dump them in."

Zoe looked aghast. "Paul, you can't. Every step counts. It's there for a reason. Tea may bring out the whatever. . . . Would you make some tea while I add the spices?"

I did as I was told. "What is this called? It sounds mighty strange."

" 'Lamb and Prune Tagine'. . . . I guess it's Mid-Eastern. Let's see. I need ginger, nutmeg, cinnamon." She was peering among her spices. "Oh no! I forgot to get more nutmeg!"

"Maybe we have some. . . . We'll check when we go over there." I handed her the tea. "Why are you going to all this trouble? Why not just give them a steak or something?"

Zoe frowned. "Well, it's . . . I guess I want to impress them. Anyone can make steak. And I like to cook. It's just, what with studying and you and . . . It's so hard to concentrate on a million things at once."

I took a deep breath. "It smells fantastic. I had no idea you were a good cook. . . . You don't do this every night, do you?" I had one of my quick jealous spasms over her husband sitting down to such delicacies every night.

"No, well, Paul should watch his cholesterol. . . . And he has high blood pressure, so I try to cook simple things."

High blood pressure! Great. Maybe he'll pop off sooner than I'd thought. Once everything was assembled, Zoe put it in the refrigerator. Somehow in some dim way it brought back memories of my grandmother cooking things when I was very young. Penny was never much of a cook. I remember my grandmother giving me pieces of dough to shape into whatever I wanted. I always made giraffes and their necks always broke.

As Zoe took her apron off, I said teasingly, "Such a domestic creature. I never suspected it."

She flushed. "I'm not! When I got married, I couldn't boil an egg. It's just you have to learn a few fancy dinners for company."

"I do?"

"One does. Wives do."

"Does Paul help you?"

"Not really. . . . Look, don't get into that, okay? We have a moderately old-fashioned marriage, but it's not . . . He's earning money. What am I doing? Studying seventeenth-century poetry!"

"You only dropped out of college because you married him."

"He's older. He's not like your generation. He expects the woman to do certain things. Please don't criticize him. I'm sure you'll be a perfect husband and do everything up to and including giving birth."

"Hey, calm down. . . . I'm not such a paragon. I hate cooking. I don't want kids."

Zoe was clipping on Baby's leash. He was making his usual snuffling, gasping sound. "No one wants them until they meet someone they love. Then it's only natural. You'll want them. You'll have them."

I felt annoyed. "Stop predicting my future. I *don't* want that. I *don't* want some little wifey scurrying around doing my bidding. I think that kind of marriage is sick."

Zoe looked furious. "You're so . . . You know nothing about life! You're eighteen years old and you're criticizing on the basis of zero experience in anything! What do you know? What makes *you* such an expert?"

"I don't need experience to know what I want," I said icily.

"Like your tone," Zoe said. "You're so high-handed."

"And you're not?"

We were out in the hall and, just as Zoe locked the door, one of her neighbors, a woman who looked to be about sixty-five, got out of the elevator. "Terrible snow," she said, looking furtively at me.

"Yes," Zoe murmured, stricken.

We said nothing in the elevator. I knew everything Zoe was thinking. We crossed the lobby in silence. Pablo came running after us. "Oh, Mrs. Bernstein, I come back this afternoon? For your light?"

"Tomorrow, Pablo," Zoe said, flustered. "Tomorrow morning."

"Tomorrow morning. Fine." He looked down at Baby. "No day for a dog."

We were silent in the elevator going up to Phil's apartment. Only after I had opened the front door did Zoe begin to cry. "She'll tell someone. Pablo will tell someone. . . . Oh Paul, this is so stupid. You live in my building! How can I be doing something like this? You're in high school!"

"Zo." I held her and patted her. "No one cares. Don't you see? That's the secret of the whole world. Everyone thinks they're the center of the universe—only they're not. No one cares what you're doing. We could both drop dead right this second and no one would care."

"Then you'd never get a chance to write your plays," Zoe said, her voice still trembling a little.

I loved her for saying that, when there were so many other things she could have said. "Then you'll never have a chance to graduate summa cum laude from NYU and set the world on fire."

She smiled, half-sadly, but clearly pleased. "I just want to graduate. My goals are a lot less complicated than yours."

This time Zoe sat on a stool in our much more disheveled, somewhat filthy kitchen while I made grilled-cheese sandwiches and cocoa. "I thought you said you could only make hamburgers," Zoe said. "These are good."

For some reason I think we both felt much more comfortable in Phil's apartment. No chance of her husband or anyone else suddenly appearing at the door. So many things were broken in our apartment, it would take Pablo a week to get through them. After lunch I typed Zoe's paper while she sat in my beanbag chair and read her poetry. I made a few editorial changes, but it was a pretty good paper. I liked glancing over at her occasionally, reading in my chair. In her apartment she had looked like a busy, competent little housewife with her apron and her gourmet recipes. Here she looked like a student, her sneakers kicked off to one side. If we were married, I'd never make her cook those stupid elaborate meals. Prunes soaked in tea! Jesus.

While Zoe was proofreading what I'd done, I took Baby down for his four o'clock walk. The snow had tapered off. It was that brief moment before the snow turns to gray slush. The park looked magical and white, untouched. On the way home Baby got a piece of salt in one of his toes, the kind people scatter to melt the snow. I scooped him up and carried him home. I told Zoe how beautiful it was out.

She looked wistful. "I wish we could go for a walk. I love snow when it's fresh like that."

"Why don't we?"

"I don't want to take any more chances of people seeing us."

"Okay." I wasn't crazy about the snow anyway. It was so much warmer and more cozy in Phil's apartment. It was getting dark out. I started undressing, slowly.

Zoe said, "I hate the winter when it gets dark early like this. It's so gloomy and sad at this time of day."

"I love it," I said. "I hate daylight savings."

"You're strange." She moved over next to me on the bed and pulled her sweater over her head.

Phil was on his honeymoon now—doing what? This? Feeling what? Trapped? Exhilarated? "Where did you go on your honeymoon?" I asked Zoe. Her eyes were closed. She was lying there in a kind of trance.

"Bermuda."

"Was it wonderful? Was it exciting?"

"Paul, come on. Stop! . . . It was good. Do you want a videotape?"

"Yeah, I do."

"Paul was thinner then, I was a virgin, it was . . ."

"Bloody, excruciatingly painful?"

Zoe put her hand over my mouth.

"Did you have orgasms?" I was entering her. "Were they terrific? Were they like this?"

"I didn't have them. . . . Now hush. Or I'm walking right out of here this minute."

"No, you're not. Just try." I bent her arm back over her head.

Zoe left at five-thirty. I stayed in my room. I kissed her

and told her to pull the door closed. She didn't want to take any chances of one of our neighbors seeing her. Then I lay there in a half-stupor, replaying the day in slow motion in my head. *I'll never be happier than this. This is it.* I've used up my happiness coupons. Tomorrow I'll be hit by a truck.

CHAPTER 14

Phil returned from his honeymoon tan and exuberant. He told me that he and Jayne had decided that, until I went off to college, they would basically live at her place or at least keep her place. "You need your privacy and we need ours," he said.

At that remark, I panicked. What did he mean? Why did he think I needed my privacy? He didn't know about Zoe, did he? How could he? No, relax, it's a general remark, meaning: kids your age need privacy. But I was relieved. Not that I foresaw many or even any afternoons like the one Zoe and I had spent together, but at least I wouldn't have Jayne and Phil doing their thing as newlyweds before my very eyes. To know they do it is one thing. To watch or observe, even be conscious of other people's happiness is another. "Was it a good honeymoon, as honeymoons go?" I asked jocularly.

"As honeymoons go . . . You kid! Yeah, it was great. Someday you'll know." He smiled smugly.

I smiled smugly back. *I know already.* But I said nothing. What amazing cool, what restraint.

Tomorrow I'll be hit by a truck. That phrase came back

home to roost, if I can mix my metaphors, about a month later, just before winter vacation. No, not literally. I simply walked into school and there was Wolf, standing, leaning against the wall, staring morosely into space. This year Wolf's been "busy," as it were, with Sonya, and I've been "busy" with Zoe. We don't talk as much or go to each other's apartments. In fact, I haven't even been going to all the rehearsals of *Just Friends*. For one, I can take seriously what Wolf said that day: he wants to direct a play, not arbitrate, even in his mind, an event which took place months ago between me and Sonya. I felt even my presence would disturb him. I'd written it; let him direct it. Of course, knowing Sonya would be there most of the time also added to my desire not to be. We have a silent but not very cordial truce. The performance is going to be in April, about six weeks away. "Hi," I said in my usual postcoital beaming way. Even Hamilton and its windowless dark halls look gleaming and airy to me in the morning.

"Did you get the note from Mason?" Wolf said.

"What?"

"About the play. . . . Have you looked in your mailbox yet?"

I shook my head.

Wolf sighed. "I think we may be in big trouble, kid."

"I don't get it."

"Go get the note. I'll come with you."

We walked silently and grimly down the hall. All I could think of was Zoe. Someone's found out. All her—to me—paranoid fantasies had come true. Someone had seen us. I was going to be expelled. But how could they? On what grounds? I opened the note. It read:

Dear Paul,
Could you and Wolf meet me at lunchtime in my office? This is regarding your play "Just Friends." It's imperative that you both be there.

Yours,
Herman Mason

I looked at Wolf. Normally we would have joked about "yours." Is he mine or yours? But now I was simply stymied. "What's this all about? Do you have any idea?"

Wolf still looked like he'd been told he had an hour to live. "Yeah, I do."

"So, tell me."

He looked around nervously. "There was a day last month when you were sick. Parent's Day. A bunch of them, mothers mostly, came to rehearsal. I think it's some flak about that."

"What kind of flak?"

"I think they want your play withdrawn."

I stared at him. "Oh, come on."

"Look, Paul, I hope I'm wrong. This is what I think. Sonya has a friend whose mother was one of the ones who attended. She says that her friend's mother, Mrs. Alexander, is pretty riled up."

"What about?"

"The sex stuff."

"What sex stuff?"

"Paul, don't be a moron. You know. What's the play about?"

"Two kids, their relationship, how they . . ."

"Okay, save your rhetoric for Mason. I just thought you'd want an inkling of what lies ahead. Remember, I'm on your side every inch of the way."

Somehow I took that for granted. It seemed too absurd to even worry about, but Wolf isn't the type to rattle easily. We had our class together and then, at lunchtime, went to Mason's office. It's a dingy little cubicle with barely room for two chairs, but Mason had brought them in. "Sit," he said.

Should we roll over and beg? I assumed that Mason, as faculty advisor for Playhouse 74, had been sitting in on some of the rehearsals. He's there mostly because this is technically an extracurricular activity and all activities are supposed to have a faculty advisor. But the other years I've taken part in it, he's been very laid-back, just occasionally making general comments. He's a short, bald guy with a moustache and swarthy porous-looking skin. Usually I like him to the extent that he impinges on my consciousness at all.

"All right, boys, we don't have much time. Let's get straight to the heart of the matter. I have here a petition signed by twenty Hamilton mothers requesting or, should I say, demanding, that *Just Friends* be removed from the Playhouse 74 series this year."

"They want it put on next year?" I tried to joke.

"They want it removed, period. I'll read you their statement. 'As parents of children in the middle school of Hamilton, we feel the content and language of the play by Paul Gold, "Just Friends," is highly inappropriate for our children. If this play were simply to be performed for the high school, it would be one thing, although we feel there is still much that is of questionable taste and content. But, as you know, Playhouse 74 plays are attended by students from the fourth grade on up. We feel it is extremely disturbing for our children to witness the kind of salacious scenes contained in the aforementioned play. If it is not withdrawn, we intend to bring this to the attention of the principal of Hamilton.' "

Mason put down the paper. "Well, Paul?" he asked, wryly.

"Well, what? Should I shoot myself in your office? What do you want me to do? Have a heart attack because some tight-assed Manhattan matrons get faint at the idea that human beings have bodies?"

Mason pressed his lips together. "That's not the point. They're talking not about *their* reaction, but about the effect the play will have on their kids . . . who are eight and ten years old."

"So? You knew that all along. You've seen the play. Does it seem objectionable to you?"

Mason looked out the window and then back again. "It did seem . . . Look, I feel the point of Playhouse 74 is for you kids to express what you feel about life. I don't have to like what I see, but otherwise, what's the point? Last year it was crazy parents, the year before Sherman Lersh wanted to throw green Jell-O around the stage. Every year it's something. . . . But we've never had such a vocal and volatile group of parents on our hands. I don't want it going any further than this. We have to make concessions.''

I was beginning to feel sick. "Like what?''

"Well, Mrs. Alexander, who organized the petition, came to see me privately. She suggested that if the play was revised, possibly—''

"In what way?''

"Well, let's say it was just about a boy and a girl who are attracted to each other. They get a bit sloshed and she makes a kind of pass at him, kisses him or whatever. He then tells her he's not ready to handle a serious romantic commitment. She's hurt. There you still retain the theme of the play, but you—''

"You cut the heart and guts and soul out of it!" I exploded. "That's a third of the play! It'll be ten minutes long that way.''

"You could write some new lines,'' Mason suggested wearily. He looked very uncomfortable. Then he turned to Wolf. "What do *you* think, Wolf?''

"I don't think that's the play Paul wanted to write,'' Wolf said in his calm, quiet voice. "I think he wanted to show Hamilton kids as they really are.''

"Yes, but that's precisely it. Do these two very overcharged, neurotic young people really represent Hamilton? Are they the image we want to give to the world? These plays are sometimes reviewed in the media. Is this even a typical situation?''

I felt like the room was careening around me. "Mr. Mason, this is a play, okay? It isn't a statistical survey. It's about people. It's about emotions. Sex is part of it, an intrinsic part. And I've already revised the fucking thing almost to the point of extinction.''

Mason looked puzzled. "When was that?''

"Before we started rehearsals,'' Wolf intervened. "We all discussed it and decided certain things should be played down. There was a suggestion that Marlene's behavior had something to do with her having had incest with her brother for five years, and we all thought that was kind of heavy.''

Mason laughed. "I guess I should be grateful for small

136

favors, huh?'' He turned back to me. "Paul, let's not be naive. You have a play here in which a long scene takes place in the virtual darkness, in which the two main characters are naked—''

"They're in bathing suits," I yelled. "They're under a blanket! You can hardly see them!''

"The implication to the audience is that they are naked. We don't see the bathing suits. We see bare shoulders, chests, feet. . . . There is moaning, sounds which also simulate, or indicate to the audience, that a sexual act is being performed. Then, immediately afterward, there is a discussion of what happened so that even the youngest kids, who might not have 'gotten it' as it were, are bound to get it. Let us say that little is left to the imagination.''

I was trying for some insane reason to focus on Mason's tie. It was black with large red polka dots. "Kids know all this anyway," Wolf said. "We did. You did. Who is this charade for? Just for some mothers who want to believe in the innocence of their children?''

Mason sighed. He was drumming his fingers on his desktop. "I have an eight-year-old daughter myself and—''

"—her mind would be corrupted by seeing *Just Friends*?" I said sarcastically. "You've never told her the facts of life?''

Suddenly Mason looked angry. "Paul, can you get down off your damn high horse? You're a student in this school, right? *I'm* a teacher. I'm trying to figure out a compromise to a very sticky situation. . . . Do you know what I get paid for being student advisor to Playhouse 74?''

I shrugged.

"Nothing. . . . Do you know what my yearly salary is?''

"Do you want us to take up a collection for you?" I said. "You chose to teach here, you chose to *be* the faculty advisor.''

"Right, but it takes time which, believe me, I could be spending doing relaxing, pleasant, enjoyable things. Being faculty advisor to Playhouse 74 is not a job with hundreds of eager teachers competing for it. It's a labor of love. Maybe I'm crazy. I do like working with you kids. I like your creative spirit, cockeyed as it may sometimes be. . . . I'm asking you one simple thing. Not just for me. It's your head. If you refuse to make changes or withdraw it altogether, that's it for all three plays. No Playhouse 74. I mean it.''

"That's not fair," Wolf said.

"It's not logical," I said. "You're penalizing everyone just because—''

"Right. . . . So go home and decide how important this is to you. Because you can have a nice little moral victory to pin up on your bulletin board or you can spend a couple of hours rewriting the play, using your so-called talents to make the points more subtly. Something that might help you if you intend to make this your field.'' He looked at me straight on. No mercy.

I looked back. So-called talents! "I'm quitting school.''

Mason sighed. He looked at Wolf. "Wolf, soak his head in cold water, will you? He's your friend. Talk to him.''

We walked out in silence. "Shit,'' I said. "Quadruple shit. I hate Mason. I hate this school. What a way to end senior year.''

Wolf and I walked outside. It was cold and clear, the sun coming in and going out. "Don't quit school,'' he said. "It's not worth that.''

I turned on him savagely. "So what do you want me to do? Emasculate my play? Make it some dumb little idiot thing that wasn't worth writing to begin with?''

"No, I think you should leave it the way it is. We'll stand behind you.''

I glanced at him sardonically. "Is this the royal we? How about the kids who wrote the other plays? They'll hate me. The actors, everyone.''

"It's your decision. . . . I'm just saying I'll stand behind you, no matter what you do. I've put in a certain amount of time directing it too.''

Ten years from now this will seem minor. It won't matter. So what, though? Ten years from now the world may not be here. "At least Sonya will be happy,'' I said bitterly.

"No, she won't,'' Wolf said. "She likes the play now. She'll stand behind you too.''

I dragged myself down to the bookstore and worked till

138

six. Actually, it was good having a lot of busywork to do. Not that I stopped obsessing about the play for a minute, but at least part of the time I had to attend to other things. I tried being Mason, seeing me as some arrogant, smartass kid, making a huge stink out of nothing. A mere play. A mere nothing of a play. It wasn't a great play. Maybe not even good. . . . No, it *was* good. It's the best thing I've written. It's just not fucking fair!

When I got home, I lay down on my bed and started re-reading the play. I decided that if there was any way I could see to rewrite it, I would at least consider it. I read listlessly. The play seemed dead, stupid, obvious. Why had I written it anyway? Sonya was right. Jim was a whimpering asshole, Marlene was a hysteric. I threw the script across the room. It landed on the floor. Just then the phone rang.

"Paul?"

"Yeah?" I was startled.

"It's Sonya."

My heart sank. No, not a lecture from Sonya, not an "I told you so" harangue, not now, please God. "Hi," I said tonelessly.

"Listen, Wolf told me all about what happened today. I just wanted to say I think it's rotten. I think we should all band together."

It was as though we were spinning back in time to the kind of conversation Sonya and I had all the time when we were in ninth and tenth grade. "I don't think it's worth it, Son. I really don't."

"But if you revise it the way they want, it'll be nothing. It won't even be a play."

"I know. . . . I just looked it over. I can't revise it."

"I don't think you should even try." Sonya hesitated. "Paul, you know at the beginning I was really angry. But then when you made all the changes and now that I've actually seen it put on, maybe it's the way Wolf's directed it, but it seems different to me. I really like it now, I see what you were trying to say."

I sighed. "I don't know. I just read it again and I don't think I said much of anything."

Sonya's voice was low, questioning. "I think what you tried to say was that two people of the opposite sex can be real friends, can really share a lot in every way . . . but that just because of that, it doesn't mean they're necessarily suited romantically. It isn't anyone's fault. That's just the way it is."

I melted. "Yeah, I think that was what I was trying to say."

"I know I acted bitchy early in the year. I was hurt, I was . . . It was like to me you were saying I was nothing, not a friend, just a . . . fool."

"I didn't mean that," I said, touched by the earnestness in her voice. "You're not a fool. I was the one who—"

"You're honest, that's all," Sonya said. "You didn't want to lead me on when you knew, deep down . . . Well, the funny thing is, I knew it too! I knew it right then. I knew it, but I didn't want to face it. I thought if I didn't have you . . . I thought nobody would ever . . . But now I see that's not true."

"Wolf's terrific," I said. I felt really good again. "He's ten times more fussy about women than me. I thought he was going to go into a monastery just because he'd never meet anyone he could care about."

Sonya's voice got soft. "Yeah, he's wonderful." Then it got louder. "But you are too, Paul. I mean it. And some day you'll find someone."

I laughed.

"No, I mean it. You will. I know that."

"Thanks, Son. . . . And thanks for calling. I guess I have to think it over some more."

CHAPTER 15

You know how sometimes you wake up in the morning, feeling great, and then are struck by the thought: I shouldn't be feeling this way, something's wrong, and then—whammo—you remember. That was the way I felt the morning after my conversation with Sonya. I fell asleep, feeling terrific about her support, about our finally reaching some real accord on life, love, whatever had happened last spring . . . and then, as I was showering, I remembered. The play. Damn.

I didn't want to say anything to Zoe. I'm not sure why. Maybe it was a matter of pride. I'd been going on to her about my being a playwright, she'd seemed so impressed by my having the play put on. Now, to have it all wiped out. Why do they even allow parents in on rehearsals? Where's Mason's fighting spirit? His job should be to defend us, not . . . But how about me? Should I really quit school? In my mind I wrote fiery letters to Mason, to the principal of Hamilton High. I saw this becoming a cause célèbre, being written up in newspapers, magazines, my being on national

TV. Student Deprived of Civil Rights. American Civil Liberties Union decides to take case to Supreme Court.

But I knew I wouldn't. Not because it didn't matter enough, but because I'm not that kind of fighter. In front of the typewriter I can fight; even verbally. But it just didn't seem worth risking that much for one play. The play still exists, I told myself. I can try and have it put on at college. But already, overnight almost, *Just Friends* seemed to have shriveled into a pale, insignificant little nothing. It didn't seem worth the giant hideous struggle that would emerge as a result. I ended up telling Zoe an abbreviated version of what had happened.

"I'm just a damn coward," I said. I was lying next to Zoe who seemed quiet and self-absorbed.

I'd expected or hoped she would make some firm denial, but she just said quietly, "I guess everyone is."

"What do you mean? Millions of people risk their lives all the time, for ideas, for principles." Who was I angry at?

"No one *I* know," she said wryly.

I looked down at her. Her hair was wet. She'd taken a shower before I'd arrived and it clung to her forehead in little damp wisps. "Don't you want me to be a hero?"

"Not really." She was gazing into space. "I think one has to consider all the . . . You can't just go standing on principle for this or that. Other people are involved."

"Meaning what?"

"Think how upset your parents would be if you quit school. Think of the effect on your life."

"Lots of writers never went to college."

"But you don't know . . . You have to earn a living. Not everyone makes it overnight. Maybe you'll have to teach. You'll need a degree."

"Thanks for having so much faith in me." I knew I was more angry than the situation justified: she was just saying what I felt deep down.

"I *do* have faith in you, Paul," Zoe said. "But I also know life isn't that easy. . . . And everything you or any of us does affects lots of other people."

I suppose it was also that I wanted her to see me as the opposite of her husband. He was just a cramped, conformist little businessman, and I was, supposedly, the idealist, the one who went to the stake for my principles. "It just meant a lot to me, having the play put on," I said hollowly. "I feel like all the stuffing's been torn out of me."

"Why can't you try and rewrite it the way Mr. Mason suggested, then? Just take the sex part out."

I looked at her in amazement. "Just take the sex part out! It's *about* sex."

"No, it isn't," Zoe said. "It's about two people who feel certain things for each other, but somehow it doesn't work out. The timing is wrong, or their characters, or some mixture."

I sat up, my heart pounding furiously. "What are you saying? Sex doesn't matter? It's just some trivial, unimportant little thing two people happen to do together?"

"Of course I'm not saying that. . . . I'm talking about your play, not us."

"No, you're talking about us too," I ranted. "Sex doesn't matter. That's what you're saying. It's marriage and money and all those solid, materialistic important things that count, not just two people—"

"Oh, shut up!" Zoe said violently.

I was silent.

"You're acting like an egocentric little baby," she said. "Your ego's wounded from this thing with your play so you attack me! Of all people! Me who loves you, who's risked so much . . ." She turned away, shaking.

I sat there, looking at her naked, vulnerable back. "I'm sorry," I said quietly.

She didn't reply. She just went into the bathroom. I heard the door click shut; she'd locked it. Despondently I started getting dressed. I scribbled a note, "I love you," and left it on the pillow.

Wolf and Sonya were waiting for me in front of school. Sonya's cheeks were bright pink, her eyes blazing. "We're having the meeting after school," she said. "I just put a note in everyone's mailbox. He'll see he can't get away with this so easily."

Sonya goes from A to Z so quickly, so easily. Suddenly now she was on my side and I could see that she'd go to Reagan himself just because my play had become a symbol for her. Not that I didn't appreciate her fiery spirit, but the way I was feeling made it all seem somewhat farcical. At the meeting Sonya took over. She explained to the others what had happened. I sat quietly, doodling in my notebook, wishing I were on another planet. All day I'd kept thinking of the stupid argument with Zoe, her turning away from me with such anger and bitterness. I couldn't bear alienating her, not now.

"I think we should let the faculty know that if Paul's play can't be put on as it now stands, we don't want any of the plays put on," Sonya concluded. "Otherwise it's just a sham. The whole point of Playhouse 74 is letting us express ourselves, not writing some watered-down namby-pamby little plays for eight-year-olds."

"Can't they just let high-school kids in?" Annice asked. "Just in this particular case?"

"But don't you see where this leads?" Sonya said. "That's saying parents can dictate to us about what they feel is fit to put on. Who are they? What do *they* know about plays? About anything?"

Sherman Lersh was leaning way back in his chair, the way he always does, smoking. "Maybe they do know. They're our parents."

"They're not *our* parents," Sonya shot back. "They're *someone's* parents. So these ladies gave birth once in their life or twice . . . does that mean they're drama critics?"

Annice sighed. "It would be such a shame. I think they're really misinterpreting Paul's play."

"Of course they are!" Sonya said. "That's the whole point!"

There was a silence.

Then Maria said in her barely audible voice, "But why take our plays off? That doesn't seem fair. Why should we be punished just because Paul has written a play that offended someone?"

"Because—" Sonya began, but Sherman interrupted.

"I agree. . . . They saw my play and they saw Maria's and they didn't object to those. It's Paul's decision. Let him rewrite or pull it. Why should *we* go down with *his* ship?"

"It's all of our ships," Sonya fired back. "It's a symbol."

Sherman lazily chain-lit another cigarette. "The hell with symbols. I want my play put on. I worked hard on it. The actors have worked hard. So has the director. . . . Paul's play is just not worth it to me. I said that at the first meeting and I'll say it again now. It's not about anything that important."

Simultaneously Annice said, "It *is*," and Sonya repeated, "It's a symbol."

Sherman looked at me. "Paul, you haven't said one damn word. What do *you* want us to do?"

"I think you should let your plays be put on," I said flatly.

"Will you rewrite *Just Friends*?" Annice asked. She looked anxious.

"I don't think so. I reread it last night and, to me, whether it's about something important or not, I said what I wanted to say the first time. Rewritten according to Mrs. Alexander it would be a total nothing."

Sonya glared at Sherman and Maria. "I think you're being selfish. If we stand together, we might have a chance of winning. But all you care about is your own little plays."

"That's all anyone cares about," Sherman said. "Anyway, Sonya, Paul just said how he feels. Why are you making this into such a big deal if it isn't to him?"

I looked at Sonya and then at Sherman. "It *is* a big deal to me, Sherman."

Wolf said, "We stood behind *you* last year when you insisted on having green Jell-O thrown all over the stage."

"And the green Jell-O was a stage effect," Sonya said. "They want to change the actual text of *Just Friends*. Would you have allowed that?"

"Maybe," Sherman said. "I don't know. It didn't happen." He grinned. "I write clean, wholesome surrealist plays."

Annice looked at me. "Paul's play is the best play anyone has written since I've been at Hamilton. I think this is rotten."

"That's life," Sherman said cheerfully. "Life is rotten. Front-page news. Let's call the *Times* immediately."

The discussion went on for another half an hour. At the end I still refused to change my play, so it was left that the other two would be put on and mine wouldn't. Gradually everyone trailed out except Wolf, Sonya, and me. "Sherman Lersh is such an unmitigated shit," Sonya said vehemently.

I shrugged.

"Paul, why didn't you at least put up a fight?" Sonya went on, but even she sounded dispirited.

"Because it's not worth it to me," I said. "I thought it through. . . . I think Sherman's right. Say it were *his* play? Would I pull mine out just to defend his right to write about the history of bubble gum?"

Unexpectedly Sonya laughed. Wolf went over and hugged her. "Hey, listen, Sonya, we fought the good fight," he said. "Let's go out and get drunk."

"Great idea," I said.

The three of us went to Caramba's, a Mexican restaurant across the park, and had giant frozen margaritas. Somehow, though I was still depressed, not only about the play but about Zoe, it felt good to get drunk with Wolf and Sonya, the three of us buddies again. "Paul, how come you're not dating anyone?" Sonya asked leeringly. She and Wolf were sitting close together, nuzzling. "Annice is nuts about you. You must see that. Why don't you—"

"You can't force those things," Wolf said. "Paul isn't attracted to her."

"I *am* dating someone," I said, "in a manner of speaking." I knew, even in my inebriated state, that I couldn't tell them about Zoe, but I also wanted to. I wanted to boast, to say: you're not the only two people on the face of the earth who ever fell in love. Then in my mind I heard the bathroom door click as it had this morning.

"Who? Who?" Sonya said excitedly. "Tell us! A fresh-man? One of those little—"

"No, she doesn't go to Hamilton," I said.

"Where does she go?"

"She's in college." Stop, stop. Don't go too far.

"College!" Sonya whistled. "How'd you meet a college girl? How old is she?"

"A couple of years older."

"Wow. . . . Hey, this is really interesting. Did you know, Wolf?"

"Not exactly," Wolf said. "I had a feeling that—"

Sonya was leaning so far onto the table that she was almost lying on it. "Tell us! Come on! Give us all the gory details! Who is she? Do you do it a lot?"

Wolf pulled her back. "Son, cut it out! He doesn't want to tell us."

"How do you know?" Sonya peered at me. "Is she . . . what's she like?"

"No comment," I said.

"No comment?" Sonya looked indignant. "But then why'd you bring it up?"

"*You* brought it up, Son," Wolf said. "Leave Paul alone."

Sonya looked wide-eyed from Wolf to me. "This is unfair. You've got us all excited and eager and then: 'no comment'!"

"*I'm* not excited," Wolf said. When he's drunk he speaks in a slow, deliberate way. "I'm as calm as a cucumber."

"An older woman," Sonya said dreamily, ignoring him. "God, that's *so* interesting. So you—what—you wanted someone more experienced? Who knew more about sex? Who could, like, teach you all kinds of esoteric things?"

Wolf put his hand over Sonya's mouth. "Paul's sex life is his own concern."

Sonya wrenched Wolf's arm away, and almost knocked his margarita off the table. "It is *not*! This isn't fair. Here I stood up for your play and you won't even tell us anything. Not even who she is. Or what she looks like."

"She's beautiful," I said intensely.

"And you're in love with her?" Sonya pursued. "It's real love? The real thing?"

"Yeah, it's the real thing," I said.

Somehow, this seemed to stun Sonya into silence. "Jesus," she said again. She looked solemnly over at Wolf. "It's funny how you don't care, how you're not even curious. Is it some basic difference between men and women?"

"Maybe it's because I never went to bed with Paul," Wolf said.

Sonya turned white. She stood up and without another word walked out of the restaurant.

Wolf looked after her, stricken. Then he looked drunkenly at me. "Did I just say something really stupid?"

"Yeah."

We were silent for a little while.

"I felt jealous," Wolf said. "Why should she care so much about your sex life? I think maybe she never got over you. I think the whole thing with me is just on the rebound."

"It's not! Son's just like that. . . . She's always curious about people's private lives."

Wolf sat there gloomily. "What I don't get," he said, speaking very slowly, "is how one minute she's so loving and nice and then . . ."

In my mind Zoe again said: "Shut up!" and turned away. "It's rotten," I agreed.

Wolf looked at me solemnly. "Does that ever happen with you and . . . whoever it is?"

I nodded.

"We just don't know how to handle women," Wolf said. "Maybe if we did, it wouldn't happen."

"No one does," I said.

He didn't seem to have heard me. "One day we will, but now . . . we're neophytes."

In my present state the word *neophyte* sounded very strange. "Neo . . . phyte." I tried to roll it off my tongue, but it seemed to stick, like peanut butter.

"A beginner," Wolf said. "A greenhorn. . . . That's us. We're greenhorns when it comes to women."

"We're wimps," I said. Wolf's face was beginning to divide in two just slightly. I tried to force it back in one shape. "Wimps and greenhorns."

"Wimps are good," Wolf said. "Wimps are the wave of the future. Wimps are sensitive guys who women love. That's what Sonya says."

"What does Sonya know?"

"A lot." Wolf stirred the remains of his drink carefully, as though it were a potion. "Sonya is very . . . intuitive. She's had a good effect on me. I was too uptight before. Now . . ."

"You're still uptight," I said, laughing too loud.

Wolf was too drunk to notice. "Now I'm free. My father yells at me or my mother gets into a dither about whether I'll get into Harvard and I think: who cares? I have Sonya." He looked off into space. Then his eyes swiveled back to mine. "Is that how you and whoever she is feel?"

"Yeah." I had by now accepted the fact of Wolf's head being divided in two. "This morning she got angry and I felt like killing myself. I felt like that all day. That's why I couldn't put up more of a fight about the play."

"You were being sensible," Wolf assured me. "Don't kill yourself, Paul."

"I'm not going to. . . . I was just talking about a mood."

"Right." Suddenly Wolf looked grim again. "That's how I feel right this second. Sonya's flounced out of here and how do I know if I'll ever make love with her again? Maybe she hates me. Maybe she hates all men. Maybe she hates sex."

"No," I reassured him. "She loves all those things . . . and you. Especially you."

"Do you really think so?" Wolf's face brightened.

"Definitely." When you're drunk, it's easy to be hypocritical. You just say whatever you think the other person wants to hear. It's simple. I wanted to cheer Wolf up. I wanted to cheer myself up.

The waitress came up. "Will that be all, gentlemen?"

We paid for our and Sonya's giant margaritas, and shared a cab home. In bed the play slid out of my mind entirely. I fell asleep and had strange dreams of being in bed with Zoe, our lolling in the bathtub together, Pablo fixing the light, Baby sleeping in his dog bed which began to float around the room. Zoe was crying and trying to get me to stop it when he floated clear out the window, in his bed, like Toto in *The Wizard of Oz*.

CHAPTER 16

I got into Swarthmore, Reed, and Sarah Lawrence, and got turned down by Yale. Unlike Wolf, who knew he wanted to go to Harvard, and Sonya who knew she wanted to go to Stanford—they'd both been accepted—I wasn't sure where I wanted to go. Neither of my parents had gone to good colleges. Maybe for that reason, all they could focus on was my getting into Swarthmore, Bard, and Sarah Lawrence, especially since they all offered a fair amount of financial aid. When I went to Penny's for dinner, she'd baked a special cake as a celebration. Seth looked at it suspiciously. "What's this for? Whose birthday is it?"

"It's for Paul," Penny explained. "He got into college."

"What's college?"

"It's where you go after school."

"I go to All Sports after school," Seth said, bewildered.

"No, it's another kind of school," Penny explained. "Now you're in first grade, then you'll be in grammar school, then junior high, then high school and then, if you're really smart like Paul, you go to college."

"I don't want to be really smart," Seth said.

Penny smiled at him indulgently. "You are, sweetie. You're smart already."

Seth looked over at Susie who was silently devouring her cake. "And *she*'s stupid."

"Hey, kid, watch your mouth," Mike said. "Susie is just as smart as you are."

"She can't even add!" Seth said scornfully. "She can't even play baseball. She can't do *anything*."

Penny had given me the first slice of cake. It was covered with a bright pink frosting and had three layers. "She's two years younger than you. When you were four, you couldn't do those things either."

After she finished her cake, Susie crawled into my lap, as always. "Is college far away?"

"Not too far. I haven't decided on which one I'll go to yet."

"Will you still come here and read us stories?"

"Sure."

"Will you come for my birthday?"

"Definitely."

She and Seth scrambled off to play in their room. Mike ambled into the living room to watch TV. Penny sat with me at the table which was still littered with plates and dirty glasses. "I feel so proud of you," she said. "I should have gotten champagne except it always makes me queasy. The only time I liked it was when I was pregnant. I bet Phil is happy, isn't he?"

"Yeah, I think he is." I assumed she meant about my getting financial aid.

Penny has definitely gotten plumper. Maybe I notice it more after seeing Jayne, who has such an angular face. "Is he happily married?"

"I guess so," I said. "How can you tell?"

"Well, like, do they fight much?"

"They're never around. . . . I hardly ever see them." I explained about their deciding to stay mainly in Jayne's apartment till I graduated.

Penny looked shocked. "You mean you're living all by yourself? Who does the cooking? Who does your laundry?"

I smiled. "Pen, I've done all those things for the last five years at least."

She looked even more horrified. "You've cooked?"

"Sure. Not major gourmet dishes, but I've kept body and soul together. Look at me!" I'm still on the skinny side, but I think I've filled out a little. At any rate, since Zoe, my body looks good to me.

Penny was picking the icing off the cake, the part that had dribbled to one side. "You're all by yourself though? That must be so lonely! Even at night?"

"I like it."

"Really?"

She looked so anxious that I said, "I really like being alone. . . . I think they did it to give *me* some privacy, not just for them."

Penny was gazing at me with admiration and slight incomprehension. "It's so funny the way I've raised such different kids. . . . Those two are together every second, fighting, yelling, playing. And you were always just as happy sitting there by yourself, drawing or reading or whatever. You never seemed lonely. But I always worried about you."

"It's my personality, I guess," I said.

"When I was your age, well, even before, everything was dating, boys, all that. . . . And I bet you never even give that a thought, do you?" She looked as though that were an amazing achievement.

I grinned. "I give it a thought now and then."

Penny licked the frosting off her finger. "We just did things. We didn't think. Your way is better."

My way? What is my way? I wondered—not that I would have told her in a million years—how Penny would have reacted if she knew about me and Zoe Bernstein. Disapproval? Anger at me for "taking advantage" of Zoe? Penny is very indulgent in some ways and somewhat conventionally moralistic in others. She would assume Zoe was desperately unhappy with her husband and that she had turned to me only as an alternative to suicide. Does she assume I'm a virgin? Yes, probably. And she'll keep assuming it until I get married. Phil and Mike probably assume I'm not, but have

153

it equally wrong. They assume I've done what they did, made it with some high-school girl, "talked her into it," handed her a line, that I'm proud, but maybe a little abashed.

"Hey hon, come on in here," Mike yelled.

"We're talking," Penny yelled back.

"Come on in, both of you. . . . You've got to see this." "This" was a Nude Mrs. America contest being held in California among a group of nudists. It was on a cable channel. They made speeches about how proud they were of their bodies. Everyone was earnest, solemn, as though they were planting wheat on an Indian reservation. "Look at that dark-haired one," Mike said, drawing in his breath. "She has eight kids! Can you believe that!"

"So?" Penny moved closer to the set to get a better view.

"Look at that ass! Eight kids!" You'd have thought he was seeing the Parthenon for the first time.

"They probably just made that up," said Penny. "Where are the kids? Let's see them."

Actually, in the next shot, they showed the woman with her kids, not all eight, but about four of them, including a baby she was still breast-feeding. "That is a phenomenon of nature," Mike said in awe. "She just gave birth maybe a year ago."

Penny snapped off the set. "It's dirty . . . and it's stupid. Who cares how many kids she has? They're all just dumb show-offs! Why can't they at least wear bathing suits like other people?"

"Because they believe in the natural body," Mike said earnestly with a wink at me. "What's the difference? What do you see this way that you don't see with a suit? . . . Paul, turn it back on, will you?"

Penny blocked the set with her body. "The kids are still up, Mike. . . . How can you *be* so dumb? And what's all this shit about the natural body? Those women are just flaunting themselves. And I think that woman with eight kids should have all those kids taken away from her and put in foster homes."

Mike grinned at her. "Honey."

154

"Don't *honey* me." She marched back into the dining room, sat there in silence. I knew he wouldn't turn the set back on. Actually, the woman I had noticed hadn't been the one who had won the contest, but a small, slender one with short dark hair who was standing pensively to one side, looking totally unaware both of being naked and of being on national TV. She reminded me of Zoe. A pang of longing zigzagged through me.

"It's a natural phenomenon," Mike said to me. "I wasn't making any comparisons. Hell, I don't look like Sylvester Stallone either. But you've got to give people their due, right?"

"Right."

He looked in the direction of the kitchen where Penny was now loudly rattling pots and pans. "She thinks I'm saying all there is to women is bodies. I'm not. . . . But if they have good ones, especially after eight kids, that's an achievement, right? Why should it be scorned?"

"It shouldn't."

Mike was on his third beer, which was typical for this time of the evening. I think he usually polishes off four to six before staggering off to bed. "I'll tell you a fact," he said, lowering his voice. "You don't even notice the bodies a lot of the time. You notice them, but you . . . there are other things that are just as important, even purely from a sex point of view. Do you get what I'm saying?"

I sort of did, but I didn't feel like entering into a long, profound discussion on the topic. "Sure," I agreed.

"Pen is the best," Mike said. "So she's put on a little weight? I look, that's all. She's got nothing to be worried about. But if I even watch on the TV, she takes it so personally. . . . Anyhow, congratulations again about Yale or wherever it is! Now you can support all of us in our old age."

I'm sure Mike is earning more as a contractor than I'll ever earn as a playwright, but I didn't correct him. "Thanks."

I decided to go to Sarah Lawrence. I'd heard they had a good drama department. It's funny, all through high school

I'd worried about this, would I get in, where would I get in, how much financial aid would I get, but now that it happened, it seemed sort of a letdown. Or was it just that the school year was ending and that I felt I'd been deprived of what was supposed to be my major triumph, having *Just Friends* put on, acclaimed, maybe written up in some newspapers. And anxiety about Zoe. I'd picked Sarah Lawrence because it was almost in New York, even though before I would have said I wanted a school as far away from New York as possible. I could justify it perfectly well, saying theater was in New York, it was more stimulating. But I knew that was only half of the reason. Zoe's attitude was a little like a more subdued version of Penny's. She was proud, she seemed pleased I'd gotten into most of the colleges I'd applied to. But she never said a word about any of them being closer to Manhattan than the others, or which one she hoped I'd pick. When I told her Sarah Lawrence, she just said calmly, "I've heard that's a good school," but I had the feeling she would have said the same thing in the same tone of voice if I'd said I was going to Reed. Is this called getting your walking papers? Yet she never talked of that either. Everything was, or seemed, the same except, maybe, in my mind. I didn't have the nerve to raise the topic.

A few mornings after I told her about Sarah Lawrence, the phone rang just after we'd made love. Zoe went into the kitchen to get it. I could hear her voice and could tell from the way she was speaking it was her sister. "Yeah, it was positive. . . . I know! Me too! No, I haven't told Paul yet. Maybe this weekend. . . . Listen, Pam, can I call you back in an hour or so? I'm right in the middle of doing something. Okay, take care. Bye."

Whenever she says "Paul," I still get a twinge, or just a feeling of—which Paul? I think to me she says "my husband" more often than not. Now, not even really thinking about the content of the conversation, I just said, "What haven't you told Paul?"

Zoe looked frightened. "Oh, I . . . just something."

"What?"

Zoe looked like I was a burglar who'd broken into the

apartment, from whom she was trying to figure out where to hide. "I was going to tell you eventually," she said.

"Zoe, what the fuck are you talking about?"

Tentatively, she sat down on the edge of the bed. "I'm pregnant. . . . I'm going to have a baby."

I felt a wave of pure and unadulterated horror. "What?"

"It wasn't on purpose, it just. . . . But don't start talking to me about abortion. I'm having it! That's it! I want it and I'm having it!" Her voice rose hysterically.

"Have it, then. . . . It's wonderful news. Paul ought to be delighted."

Zoe's face had a frozen, peculiar expression, like someone who's just poisoned someone or been poisoned. "Yes, he will be," she said defiantly, crossing her arms. She had thrown her bathrobe on to answer the phone, and it seemed fitting that she was dressed and I wasn't. It was a spring day, with sun streaming in the window, and I felt chilled to the bone.

I tried to keep my voice low, gentle. "I thought you were scared of having kids. Of what they'd do to your life."

"Yes, of course, I'm scared!" Her voice still had that precarious, shaky edge to it. "Everything important is scary. Going back to college was scary. Leaving home was scary. Should I never have done any of those things?"

"No, you should do whatever you want. . . . If a child's what you want, have it."

"That's exactly what I'm going to do."

The tension in the room was so acute I felt like either of us could have gone winging against the wall like cartoon characters being tossed aside by a natural disaster. "How long have you known?"

"Well, I suspected before . . . but really since yesterday."

"Would you have told me if your sister hadn't called?"

"I would have told you eventually." She wasn't looking at me, except for darting furtive glances.

"Before you told Paul or after?"

"I suppose after . . . since he's my husband."

Slowly I started getting dressed. Zoe watched me as though I might have a concealed weapon. The two people who had collapsed murmuring in each other's arms twenty minutes earlier had fled to another planet.

"I thought you'd give me this big lecture on abortion," Zoe said. "How I shouldn't have it, how it was immoral, how I was wrecking my life—"

"Everybody has a right to wreck their life in their own way."

"So you *do* think I'm wrecking it. That *is* what you think?"

I wanted to be as cruel as I could without seeming angry. "I suppose it's a matter of what you want out of life," I said. "If you want to be some happy little housewife carpooling in the suburbs, this is the perfect thing to do."

She looked miserable. "You know that's not what I want."

I reached over impulsively and held her. "Then why are you doing it?" I whispered. "For who? For your husband? Because he's so much older?"

She didn't answer for a moment. "I didn't exactly, I didn't plan this. . . . But think how he'd feel if I had an abortion when he's been going on all year about how all his friends have kids who are practically in high school?"

"He should have married someone his own age, then."

Zoe looked up at me with a melancholy expression. "You don't choose who you fall in love with. It just happens. *You* know that."

You know that. My heart quickened. "If he loves you, he ought to understand that now isn't the time. Why can't he wait? He's busy with his business. By the time you're ready, he'll be a millionaire and you can have triplets and live in a mansion."

Zoe sighed. "Paul, his work isn't . . . You compare it to what writing is to you. He likes being a businessman, he enjoys it, he's good at it, but it isn't . . . personal. He says he's always wanted a family. That's how he sees himself—as a family man. He's not like you."

I wondered how she meant that. "What do you mean—not like me?"

"You may not even *have* kids," she said. "You've said that. Anyway, it's not a priority for you. But Paul has all these fantasies of coming home and having a bunch of kids yell out, 'Daddy,' and reading them stories. I know—you think it's banal, stupid.''

A flash-image of Mike and Penny ran through my mind. "No, I can understand it. . . . I'm just thinking of you. You said you've never really felt any kind of independence or freedom. Now it's like you're locking yourself up in a cage and throwing away the key.''

Zoe lifted her chin defiantly. "I can still go on with school. We can afford household help. Or say I put it aside for a year or two—''

"Or three or four, and by then you won't give a damn.''

Zoe's eyes flashed angrily. "You just have no faith in me, do you? Then why are you here? Just to get laid?''

"Right,'' I shot back. "You hit the nail on the head.''

"It's probably your kid and you don't even give a damn.'' She laughed grimly.

"What?"

"Why are you looking so surprised? We do it every day, five days a week. Why shouldn't it be yours?''

"Is it?''

"I don't know. How can I? I suppose statistically it's more likely, but it's not a matter of statistics. Someone's sperm got there first.''

I laughed incredulously. "Someone's sperm! . . . Is this some contest? Guess whose sperm made it to the finish line! Don't *you* care?''

"What difference does it make?''

"Zoe, this is a kid! This is, like, a human being. You're the mother and you don't care who the father is?''

"Don't be so melodramatic. It's not like I've been sleeping around. The father will be someone I love. That's all I care about.''

"Paul versus Paul?'' I said wryly.

"Why versus? It isn't a contest. It isn't like I'm giving my hand to the winner. . . . It's just I think, given that it could be, that this whole thing could have happened partially because of how often we . . . I'd think you'd be more understanding.'' Her voice was quavering again.

My head was reeling. "You mean you're giving birth to

159

my child and it's going to be raised by that idiot, that Reagan-supporting shoemaker?"

"Stop it. . . . Who do you want to support it? Mother Teresa?"

"Me." Those words flew unexpectedly out of my mouth. At first I was horrified to hear them, then almost pleased.

"You?" Zoe smiled indulgently. "Paul, be sensible. You're about to start college. If you weren't getting financial aid, you couldn't even go. That's the most absurd thing I've ever heard."

"So, do I get visiting privileges? Do I get *anything*? This is my child and I just never see him—or her—again? Never have any say on how he's going to be brought up? He'll never know who I am, that I exist even?"

Zoe was staring at me, her eyes wide. "I never thought you'd care," she said calmly.

"Oh, sure, well, this is minor. I've fucked so many women and fathered so many illegitimate children that at times I have trouble remembering all their names."

"You can see him, if you want," Zoe said. "But I thought—well, you're going off to college, you're starting a new life. I thought you'd be relieved, that you could just go off and never see me again." Her voice trembled. "You'll have new girlfriends, go—"

"Why do you think I picked Sarah Lawrence?"

"I thought because they gave you the most money."

"No! Because it's so near the city. I thought I could even get an apartment or a room somewhere near here and we could—"

"Go on as before?" Zoe sighed and shook her head. "Paul, how can you *be* so naive? Don't you see what a risk this is for me, how crazy it's been? This has been crazy! We could've gotten caught a million times. We only haven't been because some god has been watching over us. If it went on, we definitely would be. And Paul—"

"Would what? Divorce you? Pitch you out in the street?"

"Maybe not that. . . . But he'd be miserable. This isn't how he thinks of me. He thinks of me as this sweet, naive young thing he married. That's how I think of myself. All this year it's been like half of me is doing something the other half can't understand at all."

I stroked her hair. "Your better half."

"No, my crazy half. The part of me that wanted—I don't know—excitement, pleasure—" She broke off.

I felt good again. "Why shouldn't you have those things? Why is it crazy to want them?"

"When you get married, you give those things up. You get other things, like—"

"Boredom, asphyxiation."

"No! You get other things which are just as important, maybe *more* important. Contentment, security, not in the way you think, financial security, but emotional. I'm an insecure person. I want to know someone will be there for me permanently, forever."

I kept stroking her. "I'll be there."

"No. You can't even say that. . . . You're here for one hour in the morning."

"Leave Paul, and you can be happy all the time." Was I crazy? Why was I saying these things? *She's carrying my child.*

"No one's happy all the time. I don't even *want* that. . . . Look, I'm grateful for what we had, but it's over."

I sat there, too stabbed by bitterness to worry about the fact that I was going to be late for school. "You took a long time to get around to that."

"Paul, look at your fantasies and how unrealistic they are. Next year I'll look like a tank. I'll be horribly pregnant. You wouldn't even want—"

"Yes, I would. . . . If I felt it was my child and I could visit him. . . . And you'll never look like a tank."

"If the child was being raised by Paul and me, you'd hate it and you'd hate me. This way you go off, you don't even know whose it is, since I don't even know, and that's that."

"A tidy little ending." I buried my face in my hands.

Zoe touched my hair gently. "Don't be bitter. It's for you. . . . A year from now you'll be glad, you'll see it my way."

She still loves me. Somehow that gesture, the way she touched me said that. "I'm glad you told me first."

"I am too. Telling Paul will be a piece of cake after this." She laughed.

"What if it looks exactly like me?"

"It won't. Babies look like themselves. It'll probably look like me, if anyone. If it's a girl, everyone will say it looks like me."

"I hope it's a boy."

"So will Paul. . . . Well, *I* hope it's a girl. But hopes are pretty irrelevant, since it's already whatever it's going to be."

I left her apartment in a kind of daze and decided just to cut school. We only had a few weeks of classes anyway. *Some god has been watching over us.* What god had been watching over me? Zoe had had her little extramarital adventure. I hadn't had my play put on, I'd been pitched by someone I loved more than I'd probably ever love anyone again, my kid was going to be raised by someone I loathed, whose values I despised. . . . But maybe he'll rebel. Sons usually do. He'll grow up to hate the son of a bitch. He'll become a writer, an artist. And when he publishes his first book, Zoe, by then a widow, perhaps, will say, "I never told you this, but your father is a writer." And he'll reveal that all his life he'd known, deep down, that that fat, goofy clown couldn't be his real father. And Zoe will mention all the brilliant plays of mine that they'll have seen together, and he'll say, "You mean *that* Paul Gold is my father?" And she'll say, "Yes, remember when we were backstage that time, remember how gracious and warm he was?"

What will I be doing then, at forty? Divorced from my third neurotic wife? Never married? Just a string of long-term affairs which never quite . . . Celibacy? Do I want more women, more girlfriends? Is that what Zoe was, "my first girlfriend"? My thoughts kept circling back and forth as though I were arguing both sides of a debate, but it felt more like I was both the punching bag and the one doing the punching. If Zoe represented reason, calm reason, then I should try to see it her way. She's right: would it have made sense for us to continue seeing each other next year? Even without her being pregnant, wasn't the whole point of my going off to college to have new experiences, new adventures? Maybe, like Sonya, I should have gone to Reed, someplace so far I could only come home for holidays? By the end of four years I'd be used to Oregon, and end up living there, cut the umbilical cord. But New York is where it's at for plays.

Zoe. She's just a housewife. You were being cruel but accurate. She won't even finish college, probably. She can't even type well. She just got an A on her Arthur Miller paper because she mimicked your ideas and her teacher had the hots for her. She picked Paul Bernstein. That's what she *wanted*. She could have waited. She could have married a dozen other guys. She wants what he represents. Well, part of her does. . . . And is he so evil? What do I even know about him, really? I thought of the scene in *Casablanca* where Paul Henried says to Bogart, "It is perhaps a strange coincidence that we should be in love with the same woman." I imagined Paul Bernstein and me going to a bar together to celebrate Zoe's pregnancy, getting looped, slapping each other on the back. He would be magnanimous, generous. "What does it matter whose child it is? I'm probably sterile, and this way you've allowed me the privilege of having a child whose genes will be a million times superior to mine. You've made my wife happy. Before this she was a lost little child, clinging to me. Now she's a . . ."

Shit. I'm not convincing myself. Inside me is a core of horrible bitterness which refuses to melt away, which lies there like a hard, ugly rock. What do I wish? That she'd have an abortion? "Paul, I'm leaving my husband. I'm not going to have this baby, but getting pregnant by you has made me realize what a sham my marriage is. I'm going to get my own apartment, continue with college. You don't owe me anything. Go off, go out in the world, have your adventures and I'll have mine, and someday . . ." Who's going to support her? Her parents don't have any money. *You* don't have any money! Damn, is everything in the world decided by economics? What if I were rich, had a trust fund, were endlessly rich? "I'll support you, no strings. You can have other lovers, I may have other girlfriends, but we'll meet, we'll continue to meet . . ."

You're crazy. She wouldn't want that in a million years, no matter how much money you had. She's a conventional, timorous woman—girl. She doesn't want other lovers. "Don't you see what a risk this is for me, how crazy it's been?" You were her one big adventure, and it almost drove her over the edge. "I feel like part of me was doing something that the other part of me couldn't even understand." Find someone who'll fit into the world you want to enter, someone sophisticated, urbane. She grew up on a farm! I don't care. I love her. I don't *want* someone sophisticated.

I realized we hadn't even really decided if we were going to continue to meet in the morning. I'd been looking forward to school ending, for both of us, to whole days together, walks in the park. "What if someone saw us?" Can you make love when you're pregnant? Of course. She won't even show for months, not till I'll be leaving for college.

But the next morning, when I arrived at 7:20, Zoe was dressed. I didn't know how deliberate this was, but she was actually wearing a dress and a string of pearls and high-heeled sandals. "What are you doing here?" she asked, not cruelly, just puzzled.

"What do you think?"

"But we talked that over yesterday. We agreed . . ."

"Just that it would end when I went off to college. That's not for four months, five . . ."

"Paul, don't make this hard for me."

"What? So that was it, yesterday was the end? Just like that?"

She crossed her arms impatiently. "Didn't anything I said yesterday sink in? Paul knows I'm pregnant now. To get caught at this point would be total, total insanity. How could I enjoy it? How can you be so insensitive?"

I just stood there, feeling like a fool, hating her. "Did you tell him?"

"Yes, we had a nice celebration." She looked away.

"Was he overjoyed?"

164

"Yes, he was."

"What does he hope it is? A boy or a girl?"

"I told you, a boy. . . . But he'll be happy no matter what it is, so long as it's healthy."

I looked at her outfit. "Why're you all dressed up? You never dress that way."

"I have an appointment with the gynecologist."

Somehow, at least yesterday, because I'd caught her unawares, because she was naked, the whole conversation had had a heated, passionate feeling. Now, we both stood there like dummies, making conversation. "Do you want me to keep walking Baby?"

Zoe looked embarrassed. "Would you? I mean, he knows you. It would be helpful. But of course I'd understand if . . ."

"No, I'll do it. Same hours?"

"The weekend after next we're visiting my parents, to let them know . . . so if—"

"Sure, no problem."

We both looked at Baby who was in his usual semi-comatose state in the bed. "He's very fond of you," Zoe said stiffly.

I looked at her, willing her to smile, but she didn't. "I'm very fond of him," I said sardonically.

That evening Phil and Jayne said they wanted to take me out to dinner. Every other Friday, they usually take me out to some pretty nice place in their neighborhood. They pay. We have wine. It's all pretty civilized and enjoyable. This time they asked if I'd come down to the Greek restaurant I'd gone to with them and Sonya almost a year earlier. Phil likes hearty food.

They seem pleased about my going to Sarah Lawrence. Obviously, Phil is pleased about the financial aid, but it's considered a decent enough school. Jayne said her niece went there. "I gather the boy-girl ratio is still pretty favorable for the guys," she said, smiling at me.

"Oh, Paul won't have any problems in that department,"

Phil said, devouring a wrinkled black olive. "He's not like his old man."

I'm not?

"You did all right," Jayne said to him teasingly. "It doesn't sound like you spent the last twenty years forlorn and destitute."

Phil gestured. "It's the quality. I took what I could get. I'm a compromiser. I took what was out there. Paul's going to be more fussy. He'll go for the gold."

Jayne said mockingly, "Thanks a lot."

"No, hon, I meant before you. *You're* the gold. But on the way there, there were a lot of . . . well, let's leave it at that."

I felt semi-catatonic since the last conversation with Zoe. I could line up every reason in the book why I was better off, but at night I felt like if someone had come quietly into the room and said, "We're going to sink a painless poison injection into your arm," I would have just lain there passively. But Phil and Jayne didn't seem to notice, or maybe I'm a better actor than I give myself credit for. We finished the bottle of red wine just about the same time we finished our main course. "Dessert, everyone?" Phil asked.

All they had were baklava-type things. We ordered three with coffee and then Phil said casually to the waiter, "And we'll have a bottle of champagne as well."

"I don't know if I'm up to that," I said.

"Sure you are." Phil grinned. "It's not every day your old man finds out he's going to become a father."

I looked at Jayne. She beamed. God, what incredibly, horribly bad timing. "Hey, that's great," I said. Maybe they would put down my lack of enthusiasm, if they detected it, as just jealousy at being displaced as an only child. "I just found out yesterday," Jayne said.

"How do you like that?" Phil said. "We figured it would take a year, two years, and in two months she does it."

Jayne reached for his hand. "With a little help."

The champagne arrived and we all clinked glasses. "To Paul and his future," said Phil, "and to Jayne and our future."

"I just have this feeling it'll be a girl," Jayne said. "I don't know why. I just think it will."

"What do you want, Paulie?" Phil asked. "A sister or a brother?"

I knew the right answer. "Either . . . as long as it's healthy."

Jayne knocked on the table. "I'll second that."

As we worked our way through the champagne and the baklava, I began feeling extremely queasy, almost as though I might throw up. It seemed very hot in the restaurant. I was sweating. The lights seemed too bright. A headache lurked at the base of my skull. Finally we got up to leave. As Phil was paying, I stood next to Jayne. A pregnant woman walked past us to the ladies' room. Jayne looked after her. "You know what's so weird? Just in the two days I've known I'm pregnant, I must've seen a million pregnant women. It's like they're coming out of the woodwork. Normally I don't notice them at all."

"Excuse me a sec." I made a mad dash to the men's room and threw up half the meal. I felt marginally better, but there was a sour taste in my mouth. I rinsed my mouth out with cold water and spat into the sink.

Jayne noticed that I looked a little strange. "Paul, are you okay? Let us put you in a cab."

"I think I . . . drank a little too much," I mumbled. "Maybe I'm coming down with something."

Phil hailed a cab for me and stuffed a ten-dollar bill in my hand. "Get some rest," he said. "You look beat."

"Congratulations again!" I said, trying to force a smile as I climbed in the cab. Once I was in it, I closed my eyes and almost passed out for the remainder of the ride. Last year it was Sonya. Last year I almost had someone and I fucked up. This year . . .

Every woman I know is pregnant. All over the city women who've been trying unsuccessfully for years to get pregnant are now pregnant. No one knows why. Every known birth-control device fails. Anyone who has sex gets pregnant. Men start getting pregnant. Even virgins. It becomes a major health problem. At first people are delighted, then horrified, and all the children that are born look like Rosemary's Baby. Little yellow things with horns.

With that delightful vision in my head, I handed some bills to the cab driver and staggered upstairs to sleep.

CHAPTER 17

In June I graduated. By then I was in a better mood. Not dancing in the streets, exactly, but there was a certain pleasure in finally graduating, in the fact of having survived high school. I wore my cap and gown and let Phil take dozens of idiot photos of me. Ironically, I won the O'Neill prize for original dramatic composition, maybe a little extra to make up for their insisting that *Just Friends* be withdrawn.

I never ran into Zoe, so apart from her existence in my mind, she seemed a little unreal, like someone I'd read about or invented. I slept a lot. No one was around to tell me not to, so I'd sleep until I had to leave for the bookstore. Starting in the summer I'd decided to work there full-time until college started, but I allowed myself a month after the end of classes to just goof off, eat out of cans, do whatever I damn well felt like doing or not doing. Mainly not doing. I didn't accomplish a whole lot. I read some bad books and saw some bad movies. That was about it.

One day, when I went to take Baby for his four o'clock walk, he was curled up as usual in his bed. He didn't look any different. I picked up his leash and went over to fasten it. Sometimes it isn't until he hears the click of the chain that he wakes up. But this time he didn't move, even then. I knew right away. I've never had a dog and I don't know what a dead dog looks like, but there was something different about him. I couldn't tell if he'd died two minutes earlier or an hour earlier or what. I just stood there. I didn't feel sorrow. He wasn't my dog. I *was* kind of fond of him, but what was true at the beginning was still true. I liked and still like big gallumphing dogs, and Baby was always, apart from being ancient, so little and scruffy and mangy-looking. What should I do? Write a note?

> Dear former lover
> Your dog just died
> See ya,
> Paul

I had the feeling Zoe deliberately wasn't at home when I came to walk Baby. Her classes must have ended. What did she do? Walk the streets, just waiting for me to go away? I wasn't sorry. Frankly, I was basically glad, but still sometimes I would have the odd fantasy of walking in while she was showering and her strolling out naked, not knowing anyone was at home. But I was smart; I allowed my fantasy life its due, but I didn't give it full rein. I'm not a masochist, not totally anyway.

But as I was standing there, having undone the leash and put it back on the bureau, Zoe walked in. She looked startled at seeing me. She was wearing a blue cotton dress and flat white sandals, and she looked beautiful.

"He just died," I said awkwardly, not knowing how to lead into the topic.

Zoe just looked at me and then at Baby who was in exactly the same position. She went over and bent down and touched him gently. "Oh no," she said, and burst into tears. Then without hesitation, she flung herself into my arms. "Oh, Paul, I feel so bad. . . . I know he was old, but I . . ."

I stood there, feeling an incredibly bizarre mixture of emotions, erotic excitement, confusion, some tenderness at the genuine quality of her grief, and a bewildered kind of happiness at the way she'd flung herself at me without thinking. I held her and stroked her hair. "It's okay, Zo. . . . Look how peaceful he looks. He must have just fallen asleep and not woken up."

She raised her head from my shoulder. "Do you think so? Was he like that when you came in?"

"Yeah. I'm sure he didn't suffer at all."

We wandered into the living room and sat down side by side on the couch. "I've had him since I was eight. . . . I guess he was like my first child, in a way. I just loved him. I know you probably think that's stupid, but I did."

More than me? Did you love him more than me? "You can get another dog," I suggested.

Tears were still sliding down her cheeks. I was still holding her hand, stroking it. "No, I don't think . . . I think, with a real baby I'll be pretty busy."

"Yeah, you probably will be." Then I bent down and kissed her hair and pressed her against me. I couldn't help it. That same sudden release of feeling Zoe had when she saw Baby was dead, I felt at having her so near me after all those empty stupid weeks. "I love you," I whispered.

"I love you too."

Without saying anything, we went into the bedroom and made love. She kept crying, but softly, no sound. I knew she wasn't just crying about Baby's death. You didn't need a doctorate in psychology to know she was mourning us. As I was. Mourning it, but also reaffirming that it had existed, that it had been real, that what was there was still there and maybe always would be. We lay in each other's arms, not talking, but the mood was tender. Then we showered and I helped Zoe call the kennel where they sometimes had boarded Baby in the past. The man from the kennel arrived just as Paul Bernstein did, coming home from work. For a horrified moment, I thought Zoe would fling herself into his arms just as she had into mine, and I would have to watch. But she didn't. She just said, "Baby died. . . . The kennel's taking him away."

Paul bustled around, dealing with the man from the kennel

and I said I had to go. Zoe looked at me for a long moment and then turned back to dealing with her husband and her dog.

I think that was a good end. Of course we ran into each other in the lobby over the summer from time to time, but we never said much, no postmortems. I was busy with my job and thinking ahead to college. By the end of the summer Zoe was starting to look a little pregnant—not like a tank as she'd feared. Still I was glad. The less she looked like the person I'd been with all year the better. Just another pregnant woman. Like Jayne says, there seem to be a lot of them this year.

CHAPTER 18

That summer I wrote a play about us, about Zoe and me. By the fall Zoe and her husband had moved out of Phil's building so I never saw her when I came home for vacations. I was basically relieved. Emotion recollected in tranquility. Was I tranquil? Maybe not perfectly, but I was in pretty good shape emotionally.

I changed a lot of the material. I made Paul Bernstein a slum landlord and Zoe a tall, red-haired Irish-born girl whom the hero meets when he's studying abroad. He writes poetry on the side. The Irish girl, Fiona, doesn't really know much about her future husband when she meets him—but not for Zoe's reasons—just because she isn't American and has led a very protected life, gone to a convent school. She and her husband come to Manhattan and Paul follows them as a freshman at Columbia. And, of course, Baby, whom I transformed into a Saint Bernard, is called Honey. I think that's a pretty good cover job.

In the play Honey acts jealous and growls whenever the hero, Noah, appears, because he senses, even before Noah and Fiona do, the attraction between them. Oh, I also didn't make him old, he's just two. In the play he's hit by a truck one day when Noah and Fiona, now in New York, are walking him in Central Park. They let him off the leash in the park and start kissing, and somehow he runs off onto the road and is hit by a truck. It happens midway in the play and doesn't end their relationship. Actually it strengthens it because Fiona is so impressed with the way Noah carried Honey's dead body in his arms to the kennel which is in Greenwich Village. Together they drive to the country and bury him and from then on they often visit his grave and, in the spring, make love in the forest nearby.

I sent Wolf a copy of the manuscript. He sounded a little subdued when he came over to talk about it over Thanksgiving vacation.

"I guess basically I just didn't get why you made her married, Fiona I mean."

"What do you mean—*made* her married?"

"Well, sure, it's a great fantasy. This insecure guy stumbles into a rhapsodic sex thing with a gorgeous older woman. . . . But I mean, how likely is that? It's supposed to be a realistic play."

I frowned. "You think she's too old?" I'd made Zoe/Fiona twenty-seven, mainly just to change things. Noah is nineteen, because having had rheumatic heart disease as a child, he was forced to miss a year of school which is when he started writing poetry. "Anyway, why is it unlikely? Why shouldn't she be married?"

Wolf sighed. "I guess I don't really see what's in it for her. If she's that gorgeous, why would she pick a guy who's a teenager, even assuming she wants to play around?"

"You think she *shouldn't* be gorgeous?" I was worried. Everything Wolf says always strikes me as honest.

"Right. I'd make her just ordinary. . . . Maybe the producers won't like that, but why not make her funny-looking, even give her a limp or a stutter or something, just to explain why."

"A limp! Come on, Wolf."

Wolf looked abashed. "The limp was Sonya's idea. I sent it to her."

174

I smiled. "Is that what you've been saying so far, your ideas or Sonya's?"

"A combination. . . . She would prefer that Fiona not be gorgeous and I'd prefer she not be married. I'm just talking verisimilitude, you understand?"

"Do I ever actually say she's gorgeous?" I leafed through the script. It read "Fiona, a striking, statuesque redhead with creamy skin and the graceful posture of a dancer . . ." "It says striking, not gorgeous." I looked at him, hoping that might help.

He picked up my copy and began leafing through it. "Her husband's a great character, though. I have to admit in the beginning you hate him, but by the end you really like him. He's almost more sympathetic than the hero. He seems so much more honest. What I mean is, you really understand why she stays with him."

I felt utterly dismayed. "You do?"

Wolf looked surprised. "I thought you wanted the audience to understand that."

"Well, yeah, but basically she's choosing materialistic values, she's moving to the suburbs, for God's sake. . . . Whereas if she'd stayed with Noah, she could've had a meaningful life, a life of shared passion and beauty and . . ." I dribbled off, realizing I was defeating my own case.

Wolf grinned. "With Noah? Please. He's a guy who couldn't even get into college in the United States at first. He—"

"Just because he has other interests. He writes poetry."

"Paul, gimme a break. The guy couldn't make it. I think what's interesting is how you *don't* try to make the audience like him. He's a kind of a jerk, really, self-absorbed, intense, almost like a caricature of a New York Hamilton intellectual kid, in fact. You know who he really reminds me of?"

I felt like killing myself. "Who?"

"Sherman Lersh . . ."

I buried my face in my hands.

Wolf touched my shoulder. "What's wrong? Are you okay?"

"He reminds you of Sherman Lersh? That's the most horrible thing anyone has ever said to me! It's just incomprehensibly horrible."

Wolf shook his head. "Listen, I'm sorry, Paul. . . . Wasn't that how you intended him to come across?"

"No! I meant him to seem witty and kind and—how about the scene where he carries the dead Saint Bernard through heavy traffic for two miles?"

"Sure, no, that . . . I've never tried it myself but—"

"How about how noble he is at the end when she gets pregnant? How he advises her to stay with her husband, even though she's tempted to run off with him? I was thinking of Bogart at the end of *Casablanca*. He really tried to think of what's best for her, not just what *he* wants."

Wolf lay back on the bed, his hands under his head. "Yeah, okay, maybe I'm being cynical, but the way I see it is, he doesn't really want to be stuck with this dame who's eight years older than he is. He has other fish to fry, if you'll pardon the expression. I mean she's enlivened his year, he's gotten laid maybe a million times, and by the end he wants out. Her pregnancy gives him an out."

"You make him sound like a real shit," I said. I was feeling more and more devastated every second.

"No more than most guys that age. No more than us, maybe."

"We aren't shits."

Then, amazingly, a friend of Phil's, who was a producer, read the script and liked it. By spring, they began auditions for an Off Broadway production. Despite being in a total state of shock, I went to all the auditions and sat unobtrusively in the back. I watched a flock of red-haired girls, tall, short, medium, flounce around the stage, dozens of Fionas, some shy, some fiery, some monotonous. The producers were crazy about an actress named Shelley Ames who had done a lot of TV commercials and a few bit parts in "Movies of the Week" on TV. *I* liked Jessica Wald, a small soft-spoken girl with auburn curls who came to the audition in a black leotard top and a swinging purple skirt. She looked like a dancer. She looked like Fiona, but mainly, in some indescribable way, she looked like Zoe.

The producers took me out for a drink. I tentatively voiced my liking of Jessica Wald. Jake, one of the producers, the one who's gay, said, "Paul, this is Broadway, remember?" He's a craggy guy with a big fluffy black beard and rimless glasses.

"Off Broadway."

"Those distinctions don't matter anymore. You've written about a beautiful, passionate Irishwoman for whom sex is everything, but you want us to cast a tiny, delicate Diary of Anne Frankish teenager?"

"She isn't someone for whom sex is everything," I said, stirring my drink. "She's just—"

"What Jake's trying to say," said David, "is we need someone with audience appeal. We need someone who—not to put too fine a point on it—gets the guys in the audience horny, so they can identify. . . . Well, Jessica doesn't even have tits! I was sitting there thinking: did she leave them at home? No, I was impressed, seriously, because usually if they're built like that, one, they don't enter the acting profession, two, they wear falsies, they have implants." David is blond and handsome with one of those faces you feel you've seen a hundred times before.

They both laughed.

"But Shelley Ames is so plastic," I said. "She's—she's what she is. A TV actress."

Jake patted my hand. "Paul, the director will get it out of her. He's known for that. He's taken actresses with a range of minus one and gotten them to really, you should pardon the expression, open up. Okay, sure, Shelley Ames isn't Sarah Bernhardt, but we don't want that. We want someone fresh, unspoiled. She hasn't done a lot of acting. I like her awkwardness."

David grinned. "I like a lot about her."

Jake shook his head. "Grow up, kiddo."

David looked innocent. "Me—or him?" He pointed at me.

"You. . . . Paul's okay. He's smart." Jake patted my shoulder again. "He knows which end is up. Paul, the first time, in anything—plays, sex—is always hard. There's expectation and there's reality. We're taking your play and we're going to make it into something that will work.''

"Doesn't it work now?" I whined.

"It has a lot of potential," David said guardedly, "but we need a beautiful woman in the lead. We don't need sensitive, we don't need quivering angst. This is a country girl, strong, healthy. She raised her six younger brothers and sisters, up at dawn to milk the cows. Perfect for a roll in the hay. Think of all the scenes where they do it out of doors. We want every guy in the audience to be thinking, 'Boy, I wish I was him.' ''

I wished I was him too. I thought of my conversation with Wolf. "I was wondering. I'm just bringing this up because a friend mentioned it: do you think it's unlikely, the whole situation in the play? That she's so beautiful, and yet she picks a teenager?"

"No, not at all," David said. "Listen, I had to beat off my mother's friends when I was that age. They were crawling in through the windows.''

"But those were desperate middle-aged ladies," Jake said. "This is a beautiful young woman. Paul's got a point.''

"Look, it's a play," David said. "It's fantasy. On some level every play, no matter how realistic, is fantasy. Otherwise, why see it? Why not sit at home and watch your neighbors get stinking drunk on beer or mow the lawn? Let's put it this way. It's within the perimeters of reality. It isn't *un*real. It isn't *sur*real.''

I sat there half-drunk on scotch. The best thing that ever happened to me seemed to be turning into a very peculiar kind of nightmare. Jake noticed my mood. "Paul, you're going to live through this. Believe me. You'll live through the adulation and the lousy reviews and the interviews that misquote you. We all go through it and we all survived.''

"Speak for yourself," David said.

Jake ignored him. "The thing to remember is: it's your play, but it's also not your play. It's a collaboration. It's what you've put down on paper and what King will get out of the actors, and what Shelley Ames will project once we jounce her up a little. It's the reaction of the audience which, believe me, every night is different. Some nights they get hysterical with laughter the minute someone walks on the stage. Other nights they sit there like they're carved out of wood."

"Maybe writing novels would be easier," I mused. "At least it's just you."

"So, write a novel. That's for you to decide. But right now what we have on our hands is a play, and I think it's a really interesting one, a straight-on but unsensational portrait of today's youth, if you'll pardon the expression."

David said, "I was a little surprised, frankly, that they never use or refer to drugs."

"There are some kids at school who're into it in a mild way." I felt like I was apologizing. "Just not my friends. Occasional pot or beer at a party, but that's about it."

"Not like L.A., let me tell you," Jake said.

"So I've heard," I said.

"I think that's what Fiona likes about Noah," David said intensely, waving his swizzle stick in the air. "He's pure, kind of clean. It's a contrast to her husband and his world of raunchy, semi-alcoholic businessmen who are just interested in a profit. Like she says, she missed not being a kid, and now, with Noah, she has that."

"Like you and what's-her-name?" Jake suggested.

David frowned. "Who?"

"*You* know who I mean. . . . The dark-haired one our freshman year, who you lost your cherry with. The one who'd been in all those detox centers."

David looked horrified. "Dorcas Doneger? Jesus, I'd forgotten all about her!" He looked at me. "*He* remembers my girlfriends better than I do."

For opening night, I rented a tuxedo. It was absurd and unnecessary. Phil and Jayne came. They had a baby girl, by the way, Helen, who's cute and, though this may seem a contradiction in terms, looks exactly like Phil. They say they want another one and seem almost as family-oriented now as Mike and Penny. I felt sort of awkward about asking Mike and Penny to the opening. Of course I had to and I knew they'd bring Seth and Susie, not get a baby-sitter, and that Penny would look out of place, uncitified, in a shiny unfashionable dress. But when I saw the four of them trooping in, Susie all dressed up in her good party dress and patent-leather shoes, and Seth holding her hand tightly and looking frightened, obviously having no idea of what was going on, I felt that pang of affection and exasperation that maybe only one's family can evoke in its purest form.

I don't know who else was in the audience. Friends of David's or Jake's or just people who go to everything. It's a small theater and it was pretty much filled. I had the strange feeling, as the theater darkened, that I was going to my own funeral. Why? It hadn't even been reviewed yet. But for that moment, as the audience was rustling their programs and everyone was sitting attentively, looking at the curtain, I felt tremendous envy for Wolf (who came, not in a tuxedo, but in his usual tweed jacket and chinos) for being pre-med. Sonya came too.

I didn't really even hear the play. It was as though while it was happening right in front of me, I must, without consciously intending to, have dropped a veil over myself. It was a little like watching TV with the sound turned off. Occasionally I'd hear the audience laughing, but since I was so tuned out, I didn't know if they were laughing at something that was supposed to be funny or just the actors' ineptitude. I hated the audience, even though they were just being what they were supposed to be. But there seemed something so arrogant about their sitting there, deciding about *my* play, deciding what was funny and what wasn't. Who were they? But then, if they weren't there, what would be the point of having written it in the first place?

During the intermission we all trooped out and chatted and even then I had the same veil on. I heard things people said, but also didn't, or forgot them the second they were said. It was like I'd rented, not just a tuxedo, but another person to sit there, look like me, act like me, while the real me, whoever that is, stayed at home with a blanket pulled over his head, and slept through the whole thing.

After the performance, Wolf, Sonya, and I decided to go out for a drink. Seth and Susie had fallen asleep in the middle of the second act. "It's maybe just as well," Penny said. "I

don't think they'd have really understood what it was about."
I thought she looked a little disapproving.

"Nice job," Mike said, whacking me on the back. "Cute
girl, that redhead. I've always liked redheads. Maybe it runs
in the family."

Penny glared at him. Mike was holding Seth by the hand.
Seth's eyes were shut tight but he was stumbling along beside
Mike like a sleepwalker. Penny was carrying Susie in her
arms. "Maybe you should have brought them to a matinee,"
I said. "Maybe they're too young for—"

Susie opened one large blue eye and said indignantly,
"We're not too young," and then fell right back to sleep.

"It's not a play for children," Penny said, stroking Susie's
hair.

"It wasn't intended as such," I said. Everyone should
have their mother at their opening night.

"I think you should have prepared us a little more," she
said. "I had no idea it would be so—"

"Hey, Pen, come on, the kids are tired," Mike said, pull-
ing her arm. "You'll send Paul your review in the morning."

Thank you, Mike.

Jayne hugged me and said she thought it was marvelous.
"You write such terrific dialogue," she squealed.

Of course in a play, if you don't, you're in pretty big trouble, but I just said modestly, "Thanks."

"I told you you could do it," Phil said. "What'd I say?
When you were ten years old, I said, 'He's going to be a
writer.' I was right."

Every writer should also have their father at an opening.
If they're really lucky, they can have two step-siblings and
two step-parents to boot. A full house. "Thanks, Dad." I
don't know what it is, but Phil looks different since he became a husband and father, older, smaller almost. He took
me by the arm and said, sotto voce, "How do you know all
that stuff about sex?"

I grinned. "What stuff?"

"Some of those scenes were pretty . . . Was she, was that
actress really . . . naked?"

"It was a body stocking."

Phil shook his head. "Boy, it sure looked real. . . . Even with binoculars. That guy who plays the lead actually gets paid to do that?"

"It's just a job," I said. "I asked him once what he thinks about in their love scenes and he said, 'Whether or not I remembered to do the laundry.' "

Phil laughed. "He sure puts on a good show. . . . Well, that's what acting's all about, I guess. Take care, kid. We'd go out with you to celebrate, but our baby-sitter's just thirteen. You understand."

"Sure." I'd have paid to have them not come but, needless to say, refrained from saying that.

The best part of the whole evening, actually, was going to Sardi's with Wolf and Sonya. Sonya looked really pretty, in some kind of embroidered Russian-looking velvet suit and boots. I suppose I've known her too long to react to her afresh, as though she were a woman who just walked in the door, but I think she's gotten better-looking in the last year. Her hair is still long, but she had it fixed in an elegant way with gold barrettes holding it up on the sides.

They toasted me and I toasted them and we delved into a pot of caviar which we agreed to share one portion of. "So, do we give our critiques now or later?" Sonya asked, spooning up the caviar.

"Paul doesn't want to hear criticism from us," Wolf said. "We're his friends."

Sonya scoffed. "He's a professional now. If you can't take it on the chin—"

"Get out of the chin business," Wolf finished.

Sonya was regally sipping her champagne. "Well, obviously, my main point of comparison was *Just Friends*. I wasn't comparing it to Shakespeare or Pinter. That wouldn't be fair. I was just comparing it to what you've done so far."

"Fair enough," I said nervously.

"So, of course, it's a million times better. . . . And you know what the key is? This is important, Paul, really. Are you listening?"

"Of course I'm listening."

Sonya leaned forward. It was like we were back at Hamilton and she was lecturing me on some feminist issue. "See, in *Just Friends*, all you did was take some autobiographical little slice of life and plop it on paper with just about nothing changed, no real insight into yourself or me or anything. Which is not a criticism. You were just too close to the material. . . . But here—this *isn't* you. You've invented a real person and a real woman and a whole *created* situation. I mean, it's a real thing, and that makes all the difference."

Wolf had been quietly drinking his champagne. "How do you *know*, Son? Maybe it's all straight from life. Maybe Paul is Noah and the woman is—"

Sonya looked disparaging. "Who? Where did he meet a beautiful red-haired colleen with a Saint Bernard? How—" Suddenly she put her glass down. "Oh God, that's right! That woman in our building. The one whose dog you used to walk. Was she the one?"

"Zoe Bernstein?" I pretended to look astonished. "She wasn't Irish and her dog was this mangy little—"

"Yeah, but you could have changed that. You never had rheumatic heart disease, either." Sonya's eyes were glittering. Fuck female intuition. Whoever invented it should be shot. "This is *really* interesting. Everything is falling into place. The big mystery romance senior year. Your cutting school. The way you'd walk around with that goofy smile on your face." She turned to Wolf. "Remember how he said he was involved with someone older? I knew it! Am I right?"

I was pleasantly high, thank God, or I probably would have slumped to the floor. "No comment."

Sonya laughed. "No comment. . . . Okay, well, that's all the confirmation we need." She reached for the last spoon of the caviar.

"Son," Wolf said affectionately, "you are being a real bitch. . . . How about artistic license?"

"Oh, fuck artistic license," Sonya said. "This is Paul. . . . No, I mean, listen," she said to me, "I give you even more credit, if what I say is true, which I'm sure it is. Because it means you took a real situation and you made it—"

"Unreal?" I suggested wryly.

"No, you made it . . . what's the word I'm looking for? The point is, we know what it's based on, but if we didn't, we wouldn't."

Wolf pretended to hail the waiter.

"What do you want?" Sonya asked. "More champagne?"

"Some cold water to pour on your head."

All through our conversation, scenes of me and Zoe were popping up, appearing and disappearing like magical colored balloons. . . . Having cocoa in her kitchen . . . The time I'd gone through her bureau and embraced her nightgowns and underwear . . . The day Baby died.

Sonya looked off dreamily into the distance. "I wonder what she'd think of the play."

Sonya is Sonya. Not surprising. I am still me and Wolf is still Wolf. It would be more disquieting if we had changed into totally different people.

CHAPTER 19

Honey ran for nine months. That's not bad for a first play, infinitely better than the producers expected. The reviews were, as they say, mixed. David and Jake set up a bunch of interviews for me because they thought my age, my comparative youth, would be a selling point. Maybe it was. Straight from the horse's mouth. I saved all the reviews. In fact, I even subscribed to a clipping service and pasted them all in a scrapbook, even the little one-paragraph ones from tiny newspapers on Long Island. I won't bore you senseless by quoting all of them. I'll just give you a general idea. The best was in *The Daily News*. It said:

A Honey of a Play
Neil Simon, move over. 20-year-old Paul Gold, a student at Sarah Lawrence, has written the season's most engaging and witty romantic comedy. Naturally, at this early point in his career, Gold lacks Simon's polish and finesse. Some of his scenes go over material that's already been established earlier. But he manages to infuse this tale of star-crossed young lovers with an unusual degree of

warmth and verisimilitude. College student Noah Marcus meets the colleen of his dreams, Fiona Flanagan, in Dublin where he is studying, and she and her businessman husband are on their honeymoon. Impulsively, Noah and Fiona have a brief romantic interlude which both assume will be a one-time affair. But back in New York City they meet again, Fiona studying dance and Noah starting studies at Columbia. There is an 8-year age gap between them, but Noah is, for all his youthful intensity, mature, and Fiona, despite having raised a gaggle of younger siblings after her mother's death, has a childlike innocence which makes her appear at times the younger of the two. As the beauteous but insecure Fiona, Shelley Ames makes a slow start, particularly in the early scenes in Ireland, where she seems to have as much trouble with her brogue as she does later with her husband. But gradually she grows into the part and plays the outdoor love scenes with an irresistible lyricism. Van Tyler does creditably as the passionate but cerebral young lover. Stealing the show every time he's on stage is Rob Bolnick as Fiona's brash, pragmatic slum landlord husband. We never quite know if he's aware of what his nubile young wife is up to behind his back, but this wily, cynical man may simply be obeying that old dictum: if you love someone, set them free. Fiona's ultimate decision shows us the wisdom of that.

I guess that's a good review, isn't it? I sort of cringed to be compared to Neil Simon. I hate his plays. They're such sitcom junk. David and Jake told me I was crazy. "Listen, that's gold," David said. "Simon's the only one who can get people to the box office any more. He means it as a compliment. Kiss the man's feet, if you ever meet him."

"Kiss any part of him he wants you to," Jake said.

Luckily I was never presented with that opportunity. I suppose, to be fair, I should also quote from the worst review which was in *New York* magazine. It's funny, I tend to write reviews like that in my head so reading it wasn't that much of a shock. Maybe that's a bad habit. How many people mentally write bad reviews of their stuff? Maybe it's that I feel, as the author, I know the play well enough to know what failed. It was called "Madame Bovary in Yuppieland."

186

Not since *Annie* closed have I been treated to a spectacle as stomach-turning and hopelessly sentimental as the one in which the hero of Paul Gold's new romantic drama, *Honey*, carries a dead St. Bernard two miles in the rain, accompanied by the hapless dog's devoted mistress (who happens to be Noah's mistress as well). Let's hope that an actual St. Bernard is not sacrificed nightly on the stage of the Toulmain Theater. Actually, Bernie, as Honey, just about steals the show. Whether he is fending off the hero's amorous advances to Shelley Ames as Fiona, or simply lying unselfconsciously to one side while they romp in the hay (this is literal; one scene actually takes place in a barn), Bernie displays a youthful exuberance and warmth which, alas, cannot be said of the two young actors who play the leads. Shelley Ames, whom the program tells us has appeared in two TV "Movies of the Week," has clearly strayed from her field of expertise. While properly staggered by the grace of her physical charms, as would be any male between the ages of eight and eighty, I was appalled at her breathy Marilyn Monroe imitations in the best-forgotten sex scenes. Van Tyler, so notable in last season's *Nights in the Upper Stratosphere*, walks through his part with an amiable but understandable sense of embarrassment. Male nudity, may I add, especially in heterosexual sex scenes, is almost always a mistake and is no less so here. Paul Gold, my program notes inform me, is 20 years old, and therefore to be forgiven lines such as "Until I met you, I wasn't really living, I was just walking through life," or "This baby isn't ours. It's a present God has given to us." While not being cruel enough to suggest that Mr. Gold, like his hero, look seriously at another line of work, I would venture a suggestion that his real strengths as a playwright lie in the zesty character roles he has written for the minor parts. Noah's salty grandmother, who manages to be both a card-carrying Communist and an ardent Catholic at the same time; Ernando, the Cuban doorman who gives Noah some straight-from-the-shoulder advice about women; and, as previously stated, Bernie, who gives canine dignity and playfulness a new appeal. Let me not end without giving credit, also, to Susan Fine's delicately effective forest scenery which manages to suggest that the young lovers have strayed into the Forest of Arden, rather than into Tappan State Park.

Then one day, after the play had opened, a letter arrived from Zoe. It came with a bunch of other mail, and I just ripped open one envelope after another, not even looking at the return address. She wrote:

Dear Paul,

I suppose you've been wondering how I am after all this time. I've thought of you a lot and hoped you were doing well. Then, by just a chance coincidence, a friend came into the city and wanted to see a play. We ended up seeing "Honey." You won't believe this, but I hadn't even known about it. Up here in the boonies things are pretty quiet. I'm still studying and, what with Juliet (yes, it was a girl) I'm pretty busy.

I felt really strange, sitting there, as you can imagine, it all seemed so different, so unlike what really happened, except for certain moments when Fiona would say something that I had actually said, and I would look around nervously, thinking my friend or someone in the audience would know. You made me better than I am, and worse than I am. Or maybe you never knew me that well. I wonder at times how well I knew you. Anyway, I think of you with much love and affection, and hope that in other ways as well your life now is all that you wanted and expected.

Love always
Zoe

I sat there in a daze. Love always. She'd had a girl and, of course it probably looked like her. I couldn't imagine a girl who looked like either me or Paul Bernstein. Juliet. Delicate and dark with long, feathery eyelashes. The letter was so much like Zoe—not accusatory, not even going into her emotions very much. She said she was studying and busy. How about her marriage? Was it okay? Was she glad to be living—where was it? I leafed through the envelopes I'd discarded and found the address: Wilton, Connecticut. Is my life all that I wanted and expected? Of course not. Didn't you know that, Zoe?

I'm not normally an impulsive person. That is, not only do I not act on impulse, I don't even get them that frequently. But about fifteen minutes after reading Zoe's letter for the tenth time, I picked up the phone, called information and got her phone number. It was perfectly easy. Evidently there's only one Paul Bernstein in Wilton, Connecticut. Then, without even giving myself a chance to change my mind or to wonder why I was doing this or if it was a good idea, I dialed her number.

She answered it on the third ring. "Hello?"

My heart was thumping absurdly rapidly. "Zoe?" . . . This is Paul."

"Oh." For a second she sounded the way I felt, getting her letter, startled, almost frightened. "You—you got my letter?"

"Yeah, thanks for writing. I didn't know if you'd seen the play. I suppose I was afraid if you did, you might be angry."

She laughed softly. "Well, I'm kind of glad I didn't see it with Paul . . . not that he'd have noticed."

So he's still alive and they're still married. What did you expect? "How are things?"

"They're good. . . . How about with you?"

"They . . ." Suddenly I had a horror that we would slide imperceptibly into talking about the weather and other inanities. "I just wondered . . . of course, this may not work out with your schedule and maybe you don't want it to anyway . . . I just thought I might visit you sometime."

"I live in Connecticut." She sounded hesitant.

"I know. . . . Aren't there trains?"

"Sure, but . . . Don't you have classes?"

"Not every day. . . . But, like I said, you don't have to. I mean, do you want me to?" Why am I sounding like this, like I was back in junior high, asking some girl if I could walk her home from school?

There was a pause. By now I hated myself for making this call, and Zoe even more for her hesitancy. "I'd love to see

189

you," she said finally. "The thing is, I have classes too. . . . Let's figure out a time when we'll both be free."

We did. We picked the following Thursday. She said she had a late-afternoon class, but that I could come for lunch. I said I'd take a train that arrived at twelve-fifteen. She said she'd pick me up at the station. "My hair's a little longer," she said, "but otherwise I'll look pretty much the same. I'll have to bring Juliet. The sitter doesn't come till four."

"That's great. . . . I'd like to see her."

CHAPTER 20

The next week was the longest and the shortest of my life.

I dressed carefully, wanting to look presentable, but not too elaborate. Not a suit. That seemed to call undue attention to what was supposed to be a casual encounter. I ended up in chinos, a light blue shirt, and a camel's-hair V-neck sweater. I took a raincoat because it was overcast. Looking at myself in the mirror, I tried to see myself with fresh eyes, as it were, but that's always impossible. I just looked like me. I couldn't remember what I had looked like in high school, if I'd changed, in what way.

As the train pulled up, I saw her. She was wearing her sheepskin coat and looked the same. Next to her, sitting on the bench, was a little girl with brown hair.

Zoe was looking in the wrong direction. I came up quietly beside her and said, "Hi," and she turned around. Her face lit up. "Paul!" We hugged, I didn't dare to kiss her with her little girl as a witness.

"Julie, this is Paul, Mommy's friend," Zoe said.

Juliet Bernstein looked up at me curiously, without either suspicion or special interest. She was the spitting image of

Paul Bernstein. The same round, thick nose and full lips, the same hazel eyes—it was really uncanny. "She looks just like Paul," I said, dismayed.

"Do you think so?" Zoe said. "In some ways, but . . . well, it's hard to tell. I guess they always basically just look like themselves."

We walked to her car, a new Chevy station wagon. Zoe buckled Juliet into a car seat. She sat between us. In the car Zoe's hood fell off. Her dark hair was almost shoulder-length now, but it still clung to her head and gave her that same gamin-like appearance. She didn't look different. Noticing my stare, she laughed. "Have I changed so much?"

"No, not at all. I thought you might have ballooned up the way my stepmother did."

"No, I just—I had morning sickness pretty much straight through, and I never had much appetite. But it didn't seem to have any effect on Julie. Look at her arms!"

It was true. Juliet was a totally round creature with large pink cheeks and wrists that looked as though rubber bands were biting into them. It was probably what struck me as her uncanny resemblance to Paul Bernstein, but she didn't look as I'd expected, not a delicate little miniature Zoe.

Their house was pretty much as I expected, except that it was modern, not quaint. It was on a secluded tree-lined street where everyone seemed to have large houses set back from the road. Inside the house, Zoe took off Juliet's snowsuit, and reached down under her corduroy overalls to feel her diaper. "I guess she's okay for the moment." To Juliet she said, kneeling down, "Sweetie, I'm going to fix lunch. Do you want to come and watch?"

"TV," Juliet said.

Zoe made a wry expression. "At least it's 'Sesame Street,' but . . ."

The downstairs part of the Bernstein house had an immense living room with a fireplace, a piano, and a TV built into an elaborate wall system also containing a stereo and a VCR. The kitchen, which adjoined it, was also large and very modern.

"Are grilled-cheese sandwiches okay?" Zoe asked. "That's what we usually have."

"It's fine."

With her coat off, I could see that her body hadn't changed at all. She was wearing gray slacks and a white sweater. I watched her with a sick kind of longing, hating this house which seemed like a much larger, more oppressive version of their New York apartment. Zoe sensed me watching her and became self-conscious. She put the sandwiches in the oven and sat on a stool across from me. "So things are okay?" she asked.

"Well, it's been exciting, having the play put on," I said. "It happened sort of unexpectedly." I told her about it. She looked at me with those same velvety eyes whose message I had tried to decipher. *Nothing has changed. I still love you.*

Zoe jumped up from the stool. "Oh God, the sandwiches are burning." She opened the oven door and slid out the tray. They were charred. "I'll have to make them all over again."

"Maybe we can scrape off the burned parts." I helped her and we managed to salvage most of the sandwiches. Zoe brought Juliet her sandwich, cut in tiny pieces on a plate. She placed the plate on the rug along with a covered cup of cocoa. The little girl accepted this without letting her eyes stray from the TV screen. We went back to the kitchen.

"So, where were we?" Zoe said, getting back on the stool.

I bit into the burned sandwich. "The play."

Zoe said, "It shows what I said. You have everything ahead of you. Don't you feel that now? You must have met new women, new—"

"I haven't met anyone."

"I'm sorry. . . . Well, half-sorry." She gazed at me.

"Did he ever find out about us?"

Zoe looked startled. "No, how could he have?"

"You were always scared he would."

"I was scared when we lived in that building. That's one reason I was so glad to move. I always had this funny feeling Pablo knew. . . . You didn't tell anyone, did you?"

I shook my head. "Would he have been understanding if he'd found out?" I said sarcastically.

Zoe flushed. "Of course not! Paul, don't be such a baby! He would have been terribly hurt and betrayed. How could he not have been? Wouldn't you be if your wife—"

"I don't have a wife."

"If you did."

"My wife wouldn't fool around."

"How do you know?"

"I'd make her so happy that it would be impossible."

Zoe laughed. "Men!"

"Men *what*?"

"You're all so egocentric. . . . Paul makes me happy, made me happy. . . . Happiness had nothing to do with what happened with *us*."

"Then what did?"

She looked at me, through me, into me. "We fell in love."

Zoe was, maybe, always braver than me. She said those words directly and quietly. "And then what?" I said. "We fell out of love?"

"No, you know it wasn't that. I got pregnant and it just became impossible."

"Say you hadn't gotten pregnant?"

"You would have still gone off to college and—"

"I could have come into the city. I came in for rehearsals all the time."

"But that would've been leading a double life as a permanent thing," Zoe said, frowning. "I could never do that. For you it would've been different."

I stared out the wide picture window at the gray, darkening March landscape. "Are you sorry—that it happened at all?"

Zoe's voice softened. "Of course not. How could I be? Are you?"

"No."

I got up and took her in my arms and held her, just touching the top of her head with my lips the way I had so often in the past. Our bodies still fit together with that perfect synchrony. "Zoe."

194

We were interrupted by Juliet who staggered into the room with her empty cup, holding it out. "More."

Zoe pulled out of my arms. "Oh hon, you must be soaked," she said to her daughter. "Okay, let me refill it halfway." She looked at me. "I have to change her. I'll be back in a sec."

Yes, it was Paul Bernstein's child. Checking up on us. Making sure nothing was happening that shouldn't. My body was trembling. I felt strange. I should have had something alcoholic to drink. Outside a groundhog was munching on some grass. I watched him and he seemed to sense, even at a distance of twenty feet, that he was being watched. Abruptly he turned and dashed off into the woods.

When Zoe came back, she said, "She fell asleep while I was changing her." She glanced at her watch.

"Am I keeping you from something?"

"No, I just . . . I'm trying to get her on a regular nap schedule. But she was up a lot last night so I guess she's exhausted." She yawned. "I know *I* am." Then she laughed. "Well, that's all baby stuff. You don't care about that."

"Yes, I do . . . because it's your baby." I didn't have the courage to say "our baby." But I did add, "She's Paul's, clearly. . . . She looks just like him."

"Do you think so?" Zoe looked surprised. "In some ways, maybe, but . . . Well, maybe it's just my imagination but at times she reminds me so much of you. It's almost uncanny. She can be so stubborn, the way she sets her mouth and glares at me with those dark eyes. And she's very verbal already. She was sleepy today. But she loves words, repeating them, listening to them."

Somehow all that made me feel marginally better. Zoe was talking as though the fact that her child reminded her of me was a good thing.

On an impulse I walked over and kissed her, pressed her up against the sink, my hands on her shoulders, my mouth forcing hers open or maybe it just opened naturally, the way it always had. I felt her body responding and also felt her inner argument with herself.

Finally she pulled away, out of breath. "I can't! . . . Not even just this once for old time's sake or whatever."

"Why not?" I wanted her so much it seemed as though all those other times were just dress rehearsals for this moment.

"Because it would be wonderful and everything would get stirred up again and I'd feel crazy and start thinking about you all the time." She looked at me pleadingly. "You think I just pitched you and marched off. I almost had a breakdown that summer, Paul! I could blame it on being pregnant, but it had nothing to do with that. I thought of you every second, I dreamed about you at night. It was terrible! I used to dread going down for the mail for fear I'd run into you . . . with a girl, or even alone. I can't! Do you see?"

"Yeah, I see." Somehow her speech had quieted something in me. She was so clearly unconstrained and hiding nothing. We just stood staring at each other.

Zoe smiled and reached out to touch my camel's-hair sweater. "You look so preppy, so put-together."

"Just to impress you. I'm the same slob I ever was."

She was still gazing at me fondly. "I was proud when I saw the play, despite everything I've said. That our relationship mattered that much to you."

"Didn't you know that?" I asked, incredulously.

"Maybe not totally. I wasn't sure. I thought it might have been the convenience, my being right in the building—"

"My love of little dogs?" I smiled. "Did you get a new dog?"

Zoe shook her head. "I figured Julie was enough. . . . Maybe when she's older." She grinned. "Should I get a Saint Bernard next time?"

"Definitely." I had brought the train schedule with me. "Maybe I'd better—"

"Would you mind taking a cab to the station? I don't want to leave Julie alone in the house."

"Of course."

When the cab pulled up, Zoe stood with me just inside the house. We put our arms around each other and kissed again. "Take care," she whispered.

196

"You too."

I marched manfully out to the cab, turning at the last moment, but Zoe had already disappeared into the house.

A few months later for a French lit class we read the novel *Devil in the Flesh*, by Raymond Radiguet. He wrote it when he was seventeen. He died at twenty. It was about a teenage boy who has an intense love affair with a married woman whose husband is fighting in the First World War. At the end she becomes pregnant. After reading the book I went to see the movie, which the teacher recommended. In the book, the heroine was nineteen to the hero's sixteen. In the movie the hero (Gerard Philippe) looked nineteen and his girlfriend looked thirty-five. At the very end of the movie the hero stops his lover's husband and asks him for a light. She is in childbirth. Then, just as peace is being declared, she dies while giving birth. In the final scene you see him walking away as all the church bells are ringing. Everyone is happy because the war is over, everyone but him.

Sometimes I think books do it better than reality.

ABOUT THE AUTHOR

Norma Klein was born in New York City and graduated cum laude and a member of Phi Beta Kappa from Barnard College with a degree in Russian. She later received her master's degree in Slavic languages from Columbia University.

Ms. Klein began publishing short stories while attending Barnard College, and wrote novels for readers of all ages. The author got her ideas from everyday life and advised would-be writers to do the same—to write about their experiences or things they really care about.

Several of Norma Klein's books are available from Fawcett including MY LIFE AS A BODY, OLDER MEN, FAMILY SECRETS, and GIVE AND TAKE.

FAWCETT ⬢ JUNIPER

Y.A. Favorites
from

NORMA KLEIN